The House of Slamming Doors

To John Boorman for all his encouragement

The House of Slamming Doors

Mark Macauley

THE LILLIPUT PRESS
DUBLIN

First published 2010 by
THE LILLIPUT PRESS
62–63 Sitric Road, Arbour Hill
Dublin 7, Ireland
www.lilliputpress.ie

ISBN 978 1 84351 167 0

3 5 7 9 10 8 6 4 2

A CIP record for this title is available
from The British Library.

Set in 11 pt on 15 pt Sabon by Marsha Swan
Printed in Ireland by ColourBooks of Dublin

Acknowledgments

Based on an idea by Mark Macauley and Peter Hort.

Thank you to Antony Farrell, Djinn von Noorden, Kitty Lyddon, Fiona Dunne and the wonderful team at The Lilliput Press for all their hard work.

With special thanks to my agent Ger Nichol, and also Jana Pflimpflova, Jeremy Vintcent, Ed Frazer, Danny Moynihan, Alex Masterton and Billie Skrine.

I would also like to thank Vera Cummins, Bunny Hyland, Paddy Conway, Cissie and Odie Flanagan, Bridget and Tony McLoughlin, Roisin and Tommy Conway and Mick Healy. And last but not least, Eamonn Reynolds.

Prologue

*If it was raining soup, the Irish would go
out with forks.*

Brendan Behan

County Kildare
The Republic of Ireland
1963

My name is Justin Alexander Torquhil Edward Peregrine
Montague but my father calls me 'you little bollocks' or
'you bloody twit' or when he is in a really good mood, 'old
cock'.

'How are you, old cock?' Like I'm married to a hen.

My best friend is Annie, Annie Cassidy. Annie is thirteen, just like me. Annie is afraid of nothing and has brown
hair and big blue eyes and beautiful round lips, which I'd
love to kiss, but can't. I want to but I could never. Anyway, she'd probably tell me to 'feck off, ya dirty little bastard!' Although she wouldn't mean it as she's actually really
polite.

Annie is Irish, of course, and my father says all the Irish
are 'dirty and unwashed and thieves', and I can't help thinking this any time I want to kiss her. So I never do.

Annie's dad is Liam Cassidy and he's great and listens

to me like he's interested. Liam is the best worker on my family's estate. Everyone says. Even Dad. Liam can do anything: plough fields, fix tractors, even electrics. Once I had this new motorized toy airplane, a Spitfire, but Liam broke it as he was trying to get it working. It flew straight into the turf shed, smashed to bits. Liam was mortified but I couldn't get cross as he's too nice.

Maureen Cassidy, Annie's mum, used to work in our house, The Hall, when my sisters were little. Maureen was a parlour maid and told me once about how she was always having to change uniform. There would be one uniform for breakfast, another for lunch and even a different one for tea. Maureen said she didn't mind all the changing, not one bit. Maureen absolutely loved my mother's dresses and all the parties and lords and ladies who came to visit. She says she misses all that now she doesn't work in the house any more.

Often I go up to the Cassidys' at teatime and just chat. They have great food, much better than ours: sausages and rashers and eggs and bread with lashings of butter. Sometimes when I'm in the pantry at The Hall and Cook can't see me, I stick my hand right into the middle of the pan of bread and pull out the warm, sweet dough. I roll it up into a soft melty ball and eat it. Absolutely gorgeous.

Once when I was small, I took my pony into the kitchen to get a mineral or milk or something. I twisted the pony round to open the fridge. The old man, my dad, that is, caught me just as the pony and I got stuck in a difficult position, the pony with his hairy arse jammed against the fridge door.

'What the fucking hell do you think you're doing, ya little bollocks?' The poor pony, Darkie, got such a fright he shat in the fridge door right down the inside.

My mother's a lady. What I mean is she's called *Lady* Helen because her father, my grandpa, was an English earl.

Mother is not really a mother, not like Maureen, Annie's mum. My mum is a bit more like the Queen. We don't see her much, our mother. We never did even as children. But we'd always go and kiss her good morning at exactly 7.45, and then we'd see her again at luncheon if she hadn't gone to town or the races. I wish I could say what my mum's like but I don't really know. All I know is she loves French wine and swanky Russian fags called Sobranie and she definitely doesn't know where the kitchen is. To be fair Mum is really beautiful, so everyone says. Although her face is getting a little puffy now, from the bottle.

I do remember when we were really small and Mum used to play with us, although not every day. At about 3.30 in the afternoon the nannies would be shouting out our names and we'd have to go into the house and get washed and changed into these sailor suits. They were navy blue and even had a whistle. I had shorts and the two girls had skirts. (One nanny got in such a fluster because the old man was shouting that she put me in a skirt and one of the girls in my shorts.) Then the nannies would bring us into Mum in the drawing room at exactly four. Mum would have some game to play with us, usually a card game like Old Maid or Pelmanism, and it was great but it wouldn't last long, more's the pity.

At about 4.30 she'd ring her bell and the nannies would come and get us again and we'd get changed back into our dirty clothes and run back into the garden or the farm. I wanted to stay longer but Mum always said she had something important to do and couldn't really spare the time. So I stopped asking.

I have two older sisters, Lucy and Emma. Lucy is fifteen, going on twenty. Lucy thinks she's American and really cool. She keeps saying 'man' the whole time. Lucy tells absolutely brilliant jokes and knows how to work the old man. If Lucy wants something, like money for clothes, she tells him a joke. He roars with laughter, always, and she gets the cash.

Emma is seventeen and really pretty although she says it's not important and hates it when anyone says anything about it, being pretty that is. Mum says that 'Emma's not that pretty, just young.' The old man says Emma's frigid. Emma goes to confession every single Saturday. Lucy says Emma goes so often she's hardly got time to commit a sin.

Lucy won't go to confession herself because she says the priest, Flash O'Ryan, always knows exactly who she is by her posh voice and his ears immediately perk up as he wants all the gossip from the big house.

Father Flash is called Flash because he can be finished Mass and in his golf clothes in under forty-five minutes. He baptized me. I bet it was quick.

Emma is always fiddling with her crucifix. The old man calls her the Virgin Mary. Emma hates blaspheming, especially like when someone says, 'Oh Jesus, Mary and Joseph!' But she's nice all the same; Emma, and the staff all like her because she says kind things after the old man shouts at them.

But mostly he shouts at me.

Summer

One

*If you want to tell people the truth, make
them laugh, otherwise they'll kill you.*
Oscar Wilde

Wednesday, 26 June 1963

It's early in the evening and I'm stalking pigeons, just like
Daniel Boone after all them Indians.

I love it here in the forest. It's magical and smells mossy
and it's shady and full of deer lepping around the place.

Annie Cassidy, sneaking in behind with my game bag,
makes too much noise, crunching twigs, the eejit. Sometimes
she's so clumsy that she scares the pigeons. Honest. I don't
really care as I like having her with me. Anyway I don't really
like killing any more. Only sometimes, when I'm angry with
the old man.

'Shite!' says Annie, far too loud for the animals.

'*Shhh*,' says I, annoyed she's so bloody loud and worried
she'll scare them.

'But we're late, we'll miss him.'

'Whom?'

'JF bloody K, that's *whoooom*.' Annie loves copying my
'posh voice', as she calls it.

I'd forgotten about President Kennedy coming. 'Oh Christ!

The old man'll kill me. Quick!' I break open my 20-bore shotgun, take out the cartridges and get ready to sprint home.

'Hold your horses!' says Annie. She pulls out a bottle wrapped in Christmas paper and presents it to me with a big grin. I'm a bit embarrassed. I'm not sure I like it when someone remembers my birthday, but I sort of do. It's Lucozade! I could drink Lucozade all day and I love the crinkly yellow paper on the bottle and the rubber cork and the way it pops and everything fizzes inside.

'You remembered,' says I.

'Of course. I'm your best friend aren't I ... old chap?'

'You sure are. *Come on!*' Annie and I are running now. We're late and that's one thing the old man won't have: lateness. The lads who work on our farm say all you have do is turn up *exactly* at eight in the morning and leave *exactly* at five. What you do in between doesn't really matter.

We tear up the drive past the beautiful sleek racehorses on one side and the horrible smelly black-and-white milking cows on the other, onto the crunchy gravel up the big steps and into The Hall.

The entrance hall, which is the biggest room in the house, has a stone floor and wood-panelling and is full of fox-hunting paintings by a fellow called Sartorius. There are also a few photos such as one of the Queen of England. It's in a huge silver frame and it has her signature scrawled on it: *Elizabeth R.* My mother knows her somehow, the Queen. I think my Aunt Daphne is a lady-in-waiting or something like that. There's another photo of my grandparents standing with Winston Churchill and his wife at my parents' wedding at the Dorchester Hotel in London. Churchill was my mum's godfather. I bet he wasn't too pleased when she married a Catholic. I know Grandpa Charlton, Mum's dad, wasn't too happy.

The staff and all the estate families, about fifty of them, are standing at the back of the entrance hall, waiting, excited. They're dressed in their Sunday best. The lads hold their caps in front of their privates and whisper dirty jokes to each other, like at Mass. The women stand together, gossiping away quietly.

The parentals, as Emma calls Mum and Dad, sit up front on two hall chairs facing the two televisions with Emma and Lucy sitting beside them. The four of them are sitting in a row like in the front row of the Savoy Cinema in Dublin. Now they're all staring at me and Annie, and the old man is fuming with *guess who* for being last to arrive.

'You'll be late for your own bloody funeral, you will. Ten to seven *means* ten to seven! Say hello to your mother then sit down. Christ!'

'Do not use the Lord's name in vain,' says Emma snottily. Oh yeah, that's really going to worry him.

'Oh button it, Miss Goody-Two-Shoes,' he says right back.

The old man has a really weird accent. He was born in Canada, went to big school and university in England and now lives in Ireland. He has a different accent for every moment or mood. If he's on the phone trying to be business-like or sucking his pipe thinking he's wise, he'll have a Canadian twang. If he's trying to be funny and friendly with the locals he suddenly gets a terrible Irish accent, like he's trying to be their best friend, saying stupid things like, 'bejesus' or 'begorragh' or 'fair play to ye'. If he's in England he has an English accent just like 'By the way, I went to Oxford, old chap.' Lucy says he's a chameleon. I'd say he was hairy. Seriously. Really hairy.

I heard a story about the old man from Lucy about when he was in the Canadian Air Force during the war and they had a party and got rotten drunk. As a laugh the other fliers tied him down and shaved his back because it was so hairy. Because of that, his back's now twice as hairy. That story's probably true. It makes sense.

I take the last chair between Emma and Lucy, and Annie sits on the edge. While we're waiting for President Kennedy, I grab the game bag and pull out two dead pigeons. 'Look, Dad, a left and right! Just two shots.' I know he'll be pleased. He loves shooting.

'You're only supposed to fire when they're in the air.'

'They *were* in the air. Very high too.'

'I was only joking, you twit! Have you no sense of humour? *Jesus!*'

He always makes me look a total prick, does the old man. I feel bad now but Annie strokes my hair, just once. I love it but I feel uncomfortable too as I can feel him watching me. I can easily tell when he's not happy but I don't always know why. Sometimes in the morning when he's in a bad humour he says: 'I'll see you in my study at ten o'clock.'

'What have I done now?'

'You'll find out soon enough.'

So all I do is worry for a couple of hours and think really, really hard, until I can come up with a reason for being in trouble. Sometimes I can't think of anything and that's the worst feeling of all.

So there we are, still watching the two televisions, still waiting for JF bloody K. There are two tellies in our house. One has great sound but a terrible fuzzy picture. The other has a great picture and a terrible crackly sound. On their own, the tellies are useless. Together, they work great.

On the day the first telly arrived they put it up on a specially prepared shelf in the study. There was great excitement and all the indoor staff were peering round the corner to get a look. After all, most of them had never seen a telly before. The engineer switched it on and the picture was grand, really clear, but the sound was awful. The old man, furious as usual when things don't work immediately, tells the engineer: 'Get me another set down here from Dublin, double-bloody-quick!'

So he does what he's told, the engineer, and the new television arrives double-bloody-quick and they put it up and the sound is great, but now the picture is awful. 'Right,' says the old man. 'Get the other one back up here. We'll have them together. I'm buying both!' From that day on we watched two televisions. Only one would be covered with a blanket.

The two tellies are sitting on the long hall table. Everyone is watching poor old Paddy Kelly, wishing he would hurry up. Paddy is up front standing at the table fiddling with the aerial of the main telly, the one without the blanket, trying to get a clear picture so that we can all see JFK when he finally appears.

Paddy Kelly works with the cows. Paddy is 'simple'. Well, that's what Annie calls him anyhow. The lads say the only reason Paddy has a job at all is so that the old man can shout at him in the morning and 'get rid of all the anger that he gathered in the night'. Paddy has gravy stains ironed into his suits and lives up a lane on Golden Hill with an old widow who looks after him. No one knows Paddy's age as he doesn't have a birth certificate and he collects old newspapers as a hobby and reads them all night. Paddy spends all his wages betting on the horses. Although sometimes he buys lemon sweets and gives them to Annie and me. Annie says they have cow muck stuck to them but we have to eat them as we don't like to upset him.

We're still waiting for JFK. Everyone is quiet and in suspense and Annie has to make a joke, as per usual. Annie shouts out real loud at poor Paddy: 'Paddy? Paddy Kelly? Come in, Paddy Kelly!' Everyone laughs.

Suddenly Paddy notices that Annie's calling him. 'Oh yeah, oh yeah,' he mutters, as usual. Paddy's the only person I know who can mutter out loud.

Annie teases him again: 'Hurry up Paddy! Jaisus, we wanted to see Kennedy arrive ... not leave.' More laughs. But Paddy doesn't really mind. He probably loves the attention. I can see him almost smiling.

'*There he is!*' squeaks Emma. Suddenly President John Fitzgerald Kennedy himself appears on the telly at Dublin airport in front of an Irish army guard of honour and a microphone, standing beside Eamonn de Valera, the president of Ireland, who is actually Spanish according to the old man.

Everyone is totally silent, in awe, gobsmacked. You'd think the moon had collapsed. Honestly. All the women have practically fainted at the sight of him. Even Annie. Pathetic. God himself wouldn't get such a reception if he suddenly appeared in Ireland. 'Would you mind coming back in a half-hour, Holy Father, when JFK is finished? That's grand. Thanks a million.' That's what they'd say to God if they could.

JF bloody K starts away in his silky voice, smooth as anything: '*There are many reasons why I was anxious to accept your generous invitation and to come to this country. As you said, eight of my grandparents left these shores in the space almost of months and came to the United States ...*' Blah, blah, bloody blah.

Two

I am an idealist without illusions.
                              John F. Kennedy

Wednesday, 26 June 1963

I'm standing in the doorway saying goodnight to the Cassidys. 'Night Justin. See ya tomorrow,' says Liam.

'Night Liam!'

The old man slams the door shut as the last of the locals heads home, all thrilled with the excitement of having Kennedy in Ireland. 'Thank God that's over,' he says with relief.

'Very unchristian,' says Emma.

'Oh bollocks! Last thing we need is a house full of trogs.'

Now Lucy joins the protest. 'Hey, this is the Sixties, man.'

The old man just laughs. 'Come on, *man,* supper.'

Lucy then says how JFK is a 'real looker'. I hate Kennedy, because Annie thinks he's handsome too.

'But Lucy, he's old,' says I, all jealous.

The old man's upset now.

'He's two years younger than me! Thank you very much, you little bollocks.'

*

It is dark on the avenue as the estate workers and their families, chattering away, head home. Annie Cassidy walks between her parents but something bothers her. 'Why didn't she come with Kennedy, like, to Ireland?' she asks.

'Who's that?' asks Maureen back, still happy and dreaming of President Kennedy and how it's so amazing that Kennedy is, at that very moment, standing on the same soil and not so very far away either.

'Jackie? Mrs Kennedy,' says Annie.

Liam Cassidy, ever the diplomat, explains: 'Well Annie, she probably felt it was his thing, the Irish connection and all, the special thing to him, so to speak. You know that kind of a way? She didn't want to interfere.'

'I'm not so sure,' says Maureen, suspicious. 'He normally takes her everywhere. And she doesn't look so happy in her photo shots any more.'

'You read too many of those gossipy magazines,' says Liam.

'Well, does she? You don't always have to marry the right person you know, like from the same background. You should only marry for love.'

Liam smiles.

*

It's supper and we're all sucking asparagus and Mum is being interesting for once and telling us all about her friends the Kennedys, when she knew them in London before the war. Apparently JFK's old man, Joe, was the American ambassador to England.

Bridget Collins, one of our parlour maids who comes from County Carlow and is my best friend apart from Annie, is pouring Mum her usual bucket of wine. Bridget practically spills the wine in the excitement of hearing Mum yak on about JF bloody K and how well she knew him. Emma as usual wants to add a religious tone. 'Exciting about Kennedy, Bridget, isn't it?'

'Oh God, yes, Emma. It is.'

'He's not America's *first* Irish president, you know,' says Emma, all clever.

'You're codding.' Bridget is stunned.

'He's their first *Roman Catholic*, Irish president.'

'I never.'

'Bridget fancies his pants,' says Lucy.

'I do not!'

'You do so.' Bridget blushes and looks thrilled. Meanwhile I open Annie's present on the table so I can drink it. Everyone is shocked to find out it's my birthday. They are all embarrassed they haven't remembered, except the old man. He's just furious that I didn't tell him, as though I'm trying to make him look bad. The good thing is he then orders Bridget to get some champagne, non-vintage of course, so we can all celebrate. He even asks how old I am. I love the attention. Everyone's being nice to me. The other time I get attention is when I'm ill. For some strange reason, the parentals make sure we are really looked after when we're sick and for once don't give us a hard time.

Mum, now full of French bubbles, goes blathering on about her good friends the Kennedys and how my uncle Freddie, Mum's brother, fell in love with Kick Kennedy, JFK's sister. Sadly for uncle Freddie, Kick married an English fella, William Cavendish. But he was shot in the war by a German sniper. Then Kick was going to marry a Lord Peter Fitz-something-or-other but they were both killed in a plane crash. Mum says they were flying to see Kick's mother, to try and get her permission to marry. Obviously they never made it.

Mum went to Kick's funeral at Farm Street Church in London, right behind the Dorchester Hotel. JFK didn't go and neither did the rest of the family, apart from their father Joe who was a right old criminal, according to the old man. Apparently Rose Kennedy, the mother, wouldn't let anyone go to see Kick buried because Kick had disobeyed her and was going to marry a Protestant.

'That's *appalling!*' says Emma, horrified at the idea that a Catholic woman could do such a thing.

The old man then swings the whole conversation round to himself as bloody usual. 'It happened to us as well, just the other way round. Your grandfather, the Earl of bloody Charlton, God rest his soul, refused to give your mother away. Wouldn't step foot inside a papist church. Waited outside with Winston bloody Churchill. Your grandfather couldn't stand the sight of me just because I was a Catholic. Can you believe it?'

'That's not true, darling. My dear Papa just thought you were perhaps a little wild. *The wild colonial boy*, that's what he named you. I was thrilled!' says Mum, beaming away, although the vino probably helped.

'Well, I've responsibilities now, haven't I?' It's odd but I'm sure I see Mum raise her eyebrows at what the old man has just said. I can always tell when something winds her up, but I don't know what it is, not this time. Mum's dad, the earl, told his children that it was never good to show too much emotion. One thing you can say about Mum: she never disobeyed her dad. Not on that count anyway.

Bridget is still fiddling around with dishes at the sideboard pretending to work just so she can listen. The old man notices. 'All right, Bridget. Off you go. The children will clear.'

'Yes, sir. Thank you, sir. Good night, m'lady.'

'Good night, Bridget.'

I like Bridget. She's a laugh and really pretty and curvy although a bit old now, at least twenty-two. 'Thanks Bridge, good night.'

'Happy birthday, pet.' Bridget leaves and the old man jumps up and goes to the door. He isn't small, the old man. He's quite a heavy old bollocks. Lucy says he *lumbers*. Not only that but he has these big hairy eyebrows that stick out. Disgusting. Like an ant when you look at it through a magnifying glass.

The old man checks outside, locks the door, then sits down and coughs. Oh fuck, what now? He always coughs when he's about to make an announcement of national importance. 'Now, Justin? Your mother and I have had a chat. We want you to invite friends over, you know, from school.' What the fuck is he on about?

'I don't have friends at school.'

Mum joins in, a team effort. 'Darling? You're exaggerating. I'm sure you have *lots* of friends.'

'Mother?' She hates being called *Mother*. 'I go to school in England. Remember?'

'They can get a ticket. I'll send one. Your mother and I'll be happy to pay,' says the old man, all enthusiastic about his brilliant idea.

'What's the point? I don't like them, snotty English boys.'

The old man's finished being all reasonable and persuasive. 'The point is, you go to school in England to try and turn you into an English gentlemen, therefore it would be fitting if you had boys of that type to muck around with.'

'Who says?'

'*I* say!'

Emma, brain working overtime, suddenly clicks. 'You don't like Annie.'

Jesus Christ. All hell breaks loose as Emma and Lucy attack the parentals about how they think all the Irish are thieves and the old man really upsets Lucy about her last boyfriend Paddy Cusack, a stable lad from County Cavan, by insisting that he almost certainly stole some of their silver candlesticks. The one time Lucy and Emma dare to really take on the parents is about me. Somehow they always manage to make it look as though it's about them. I just sit there watching as they all have a go at each other, until I've had enough. 'Oh, *shut up!*' I shout really loud. Everyone stops, stunned that Justin has dared to speak.

'Thank you. Well done,' says Emma, all righteous.

'All of you! ... Why is the argument always about me?'

Emma's absolutely indignant. 'That's so unfair. I'm just standing up for you.'

And so is Lucy, indignant too. 'So am I. So ungrateful, man.' The old man has the last word. 'The point is that, from this day on, I will not have children of the staff in my house. Understood?'

'Yes, Dad, I understand.' *You big fecking bully!* I hate you, I do. More than anything in the whole world. 'May I get down, please?' ... Before I do something I regret like smashing the empty Lucozade bottle over your big fat hairy head.

He's happy with himself having won the day. 'Good boy. Off you go then.' I'm walking down the bedroom passage now and I'm so fucking angry with my *pathetic cowardliness* that I kick the curtains. It's too late and too dark to go out into the forest and shoot something. Although I don't know why I do it as I always feel bad afterwards. I remember once after the old man had upset me and I was really angry, I blasted this tiny rabbit, a baby not big enough to eat. When I got to it, it was still alive and looking up to me for help with its sad little eyes. I swear it was crying. I bashed it over the head with the butt of my gun to put it out of its misery. I never told anyone and I still feel bad even though it was at least two years ago.

Suddenly I hear pop music: '*Love, love me do.*' It's The Beatles, that group Lucy is mad about. I see Bridget and she hasn't seen me. She's in a blue dressing gown and carrying her new, flashy, Silvertone transistor radio. She slips into the bathroom in her bare feet and closes the door. I stalk up, commando-like, and kneeling down, peer through the keyhole and watch and listen. '*So, please love me do. Love me do.*' Bridget removes her dressing gown and suddenly I realize why men fall in love. I've never seen breasts in real life, not even Mother's. The old man has *Playboy* magazine which he sneaks into Ireland, hidden away from the customs officers. He really loves looking at black girls and their big 'bubbly doops' as he calls them. He hides the magazine in the cover of *Country Life*. But I always manage to find it.

There they were, *oh my God,* Bridget's incredible bubbly doops and they are really the most beautiful things I have ever seen in my life. I can't think straight, all the anger has left me and I just want to burst in, climb all over her and bury my head in them.

*

Downstairs, Lucy Montague is washing the Renaissance Gold Wedgwood coffee cups in the pantry sink. Emma, drying, roughly snatches a saucer from Lucy's hand. 'Steady!' says Lucy, mystified by Emma's aggressive behaviour.

'Sorry,' says Emma. 'I can't help it. He'd be fine, Dad, on his own. She just puts these ideas into his head because she's bored and wants to cause trouble. Why does he do it?'

'Do what?'

'Just do everything she says?'

'Ah. First, she's on a pedestal way above him, up in the sky. She's got a handle, man ...'

Emma, confused, interrupts. 'A handle?'

'A title. Lady Helen? That makes her much posher. It
makes him insecure.'
  'And second?'
  'Secondly, the dosh ... she has it. He doesn't.'
  'So?'
  'What do they say in west Cork? "Money talks. But if
you marry it, it never shuts up!"'
  Emma's mask falls. She laughs.

*

I'm running my bath but I can't stop thinking about Bridget's breasts and Annie's lips. They've all become one, a blur.
I have a photo of Annie stuck on my long dressing-mirror,
grinning away with her lovely big lips. I better hide it from
the old man or he'll have it removed. 'We cannot have photographs of children of the staff in this house. I will not allow
it!' Oh I get you, you tosser! It's all right to have *Playboy*
photos of darkie breasts all over the place but not a normal
one of my friend, *with* her clothes on, you fecking perv!
  I'm staring at Annie's photo and I'm wondering what it
would be like to kiss it so I lick it instead and I'm still thinking of Bridget's boobs and what it would be like to lick them.
Shit. Now I feel bad. Lucy says I'm full of Catholic guilt,
whatever that is.
  Suddenly I'm angry again and I look in the long mirror
and I look fat and I pull all the spare bits of flesh but they
won't come off. 'Feck, feck, *feck!*' How on God's earth am I
going to explain to Annie about her being banned from my
house? And what will Maureen say?
  Maureen Cassidy is one of the few local people who likes
Mum. I think that's because Maureen only sees the glamour
and the dresses and that sort of thing. When Maureen worked

in our house years ago, Mum was not so far into the drink and was a little bit nicer and obviously looked better, not so puffy. One night when I was at the Cassidys' house watching them eat their yummy tea, Maureen told me about the parties when I was a baby and before I was born.

'There used to be these great dinner parties, really fantastic! All these lords and ladies came and the women were all a bit jealous of your mother because all the men were staring at her because she was so beautiful. Of course all these people were posh, the ones that came to the dinners, but they didn't have the same kind of money as your parents, Justin. The women were dressed in clothes from Dunnes' Stores or Switzers. But your mother, she wasn't. She was dressed in Christian Dior and Sibyl Connelly and she looked beautiful, oh my God, she really did. Your father was jealous as well and one night he took a carving knife to one of the guests for staring at your mother. Anyways, the next day your father comes into the kitchen and tells us all, the staff, "I goddamned took a carving knife to that Mr bloody Cooper last night for making eyes at my bloody wife! He won't be showing his face around here so often, I can tell you."'

Maureen says that people get a little disappointed with Mum because she doesn't pay enough attention to the families of the workers any more. Apparently it is normal for the lady of the house to show an interest in the families' welfare. Just to go around and chat to everyone and let them know she cares about them. Mum used to be quite good at this, according to Maureen, until she started drinking.

Una Kershaw, who was the head nanny when I was born, recently told me the same sort of thing. 'She didn't start with the drinking, Her Ladyship, until she thought she was starting to lose her looks,' said Una. 'And Emma was getting to be a real looker and the boys were all gawping at her and your mother didn't like that as she was always the prettiest woman around and she's not any more and she has to have a drink to make her feel better. Of course the drink is doing the opposite and it'll ruin her looks, more's the pity.'

Una was right about this and this is how I know. I remember a couple of years ago when Lucy and Emma arrived back from school and Emma was then fifteen. I was shocked at how lovely she had become. I almost forgot she was my sister and used to dream about her at night. Really. I couldn't help it. She was dead sexy.

Mum didn't want anyone around the house who looked as good as her. And Emma did. Everyone, but everyone, was saying how beautiful Emma was with her shiny long dark hair and her lovely skin and great curvy figure and the fact that she looked so natural. So Mum, of course, was not happy. She was jealous of all the attention that Emma got, especially from the old man, but she pretended to be happy and kept telling Emma how proud she was. Lying cow.

Mum persuaded Emma, who was very innocent, that she should take her as a special treat to get her hair done at Brown Thomas, Dublin's version of Harrods. Off they went to Dublin, Emma full of delight with herself. When they came back a few hours later Emma looked white in the face and bleary-eyed from crying. Her hair was absolutely ruined.

Mum had convinced Emma that her hair should be permed as 'it looks a little dull, darling'. Perming it would 'give it some life and make you look much more grown-up'. Emma fell for it. By the time she twigged what was happening it was too late and it took a year for her hair to become long and natural again. I didn't really hate Mum, not like I did the old man, but I came close to it that particular time.

But then, Emma is naive, very naive. She always expects Mum to be kind to her and is always disappointed. As for myself, I don't really get upset with Mum, because truthfully I hardly know her. I mean, Mum never looked after us as babies and if I didn't have to go and kiss her good morning, I would hardly see her at all. But for the girls it's different. It is like a permanent battle and they really, really despise her.

In the old days when Mum wasn't drinking so much, we used to have an estate Christmas party. All the parents would bring their children into our schoolhouse, where my sisters and me used to be taught by the governess before we went to big school in England. There would be a great social with ice cream and cakes and Lucozade and all sorts of games, which Mum would organize. At the end Mum used to give out presents. She loved doing it. There was an old stable door at the back of the schoolhouse and she would hide behind it with all the presents and a fishing rod. Mum, hidden away, would dangle a wrapped present over the half-door using the rod and would then call out the name of a child who would walk forward and take their present. That was really good fun. She doesn't do those things any more.

More often than not I made my own toys. Most people thought, especially anyone English, that you could just buy what you wanted if you had money. Not in Ireland. Once when I was about eight years old I saw this film about robots, *The Day the Earth Stood Still*. I decided then and there that this was what I wanted to be: a shiny robot. So I got a few old cardboard boxes and strung them together. I had three boxes all tied up with string, one on top of the other.

Then off I went to Dublin on the most important part of the exercise. It took half a day to find a little pot of silver paint but it was worth the long search. I was thrilled. When I got home I painted the three boxes, made slits for eyes, and transformed myself into a fully fledged robot. I walked around, peering wildly through the slits, trying to terrify everyone.

Three

An Anglo-Irishman is a Protestant with a horse.

Brendan Behan

Thursday, 27 June 1963

I'm dreaming and it's horrible and all I can hear is this loud voice, roaring away: 'Paddy! Paddy, *Padddyyy?*' I'm awake now and the morning sun peeks annoyingly through my skinny curtains, and I can still hear the yelling: 'Paddy! Paddy? *Padddyyy?*' Fuck! I know exactly where it's coming from.

The old man is outside the milking parlour across the yard and he's 'relieving all the anger he gathered in the night'. He's screaming for poor Paddy and now I'm covering my ears as I can't bear to listen and I'm too scared to go out there and defend him. I should do it and I'm ashamed, but I just can't. The old man would kill me.

*

Inside the milking parlour, life continues as normal. 'Come here, you!'

Bobby Montague, purple with rage, grabs Paddy Kelly's

coat collar and pushes his face right down into a large, empty milk churn.

'In there, look! Bits stuck everywhere. How many times do I have to tell you? First, wash it in cold water to separate the fat from the protein. Then, only then, you wash it in hot. Not the other way round, you useless Irish cunt!'

*

I'm on Night Train, our best racehorse, and we're cantering round the long meadow, three horses all in a line. Well, we're supposed to be cantering as the horses are only just in from the grass and still fat but I'm exploding inside and I'm making him really move his arse and I'm slapping him down the shoulder.

'Geww on! Geww on!' I yell at him, lying crouched over his withers. I squeeze as hard as I can with my knees and he starts to gallop, really fly, and he's starting to blow now and Danny, the head stable lad, is yelling from behind.

'Hey Justin, steady, steady!' But I don't give a shite and I keep going.

A little later there we all are, standing in the clear brown river with the water rushing past over the horses' knees. It's really good for their shins, this swirly water, and it's great to see all the minnows gather round the horses' legs, nibbling away at God-knows-what. I've undone the saddle girth a couple of holes to let Night Train breathe and the sweat dry and I have my legs out of my stirrups and let them hang right down and I take a Player's fag with the lads as the annoying midges and flies circle us.

Night Train starts to paw the water – pat, pat, splash – and I know he wants to have a roll so I give him a kick so he knows I won't have it. No thanks. I'm not wearing my trunks. Next thing I know he's forgotten the kick and is twisting his head round practically munching my jodhpur boots, looking back at me, pleading for sugar. So I delve into my pocket and pull out a couple of lumps. He's happy now and slobbers them right off my outstretched palm.

*

Bobby Montague stands at the front door of The Hall, looking out for someone. He still wears his milking clothes: a cream-coloured Norwegian jumper, dark-green corduroy trousers but no gumboots, just long red shooting socks. Bobby checks his watch and talks to himself, 'A quarter to eight, exactly ... little bollocks.'

Now he's yelling, 'Justin? Oi, Justin!' There is no answer and Bobby, wishing he didn't hate the boy so much, strides back inside, slamming the door.

*

I'm on my way back from the stables and I'm still riding but this time it's my bike and I'm riding the winner of the Epsom Derby and I'm late for breakfast and I still don't give a shite. I'd make a great racing commentator. *'Yes, it really must be Larkspur now. Arcor and Le Cantilien haven't a hope in catching him ... Larkspur wins the Derby for Ireland!'* I lepp off the bike and it clatters against the wall and I run in quick as anything to kiss Her Majesty good morning.

I'm standing in Mum's bedroom and I know I'm going to be late for breakfast as the clock already says six past eight and I'll be in big trouble as usual. She's on the telephone. Everyone says how friendly we all are in Ireland but I'm not so sure. I think we're all just bloody nosy.

I spin my whip like Scobie Breasley, the great Australian jockey, and I stare at Her Majesty's untouched grapefruit with the stupid cherry stuck on top, sitting centre stage on that ridiculous wicker breakfast tray, and I stare at her nodding head and I listen. She hasn't seen me, and she's still yakking away. 'Well, he was a wild colonial when we married even though he'd been to Oxford. Almost uncontrollable and much, much more interesting than those stuck-up, self-important old Etonians. He really was.' She takes her small, *secret she thinks*, hip-flask and pours the vodka into the orange juice and she doesn't know I'm watching. 'I don't know what's changed him. But frankly, Joan, I'm getting a little tired of it. I feel like doing something really outrageous, just for a reaction. Ha, ha!'

'*Ha, ha!*' says I, surprising her. She's shocked to see me and looks worried.

'You shouldn't eavesdrop.'

'Good morning, *Mother*.'

'*Mummy*, call me Mummy. By the way, have you seen my cigarette case? The gold one. Your father's lovely wedding present.'

'Nope.' I kiss her quick as it feels so weird and I leave. Why do I have to kiss her? It's really odd. Mum has never, ever, kissed us. We always have to kiss her first.

*

Annie Cassidy is on her way out through the main gates of The Hall, which are right at the end of the long avenue, about half a mile from the main house. Annie is off to fetch her mother's messages from Crauls, the local shop. She is content, very content. She had a wonderful night, dreaming of how she kissed President Kennedy, and how he loved it.

She won't tell Justin. She knows how jealous he gets.

Annie swings the shopping bag, which clinks with empty bottles and sings that summer's number-one hit: 'It's my party, and I'll cry if I want to, cry if I want to. You would cry too, if it happened to you. Do, do, do … hello?' Annie stops dead in her tracks and stares with delight. A green MGB sports car pulls up with its hood down. The driver is a man of about forty. He is handsome in a rakish sort of way. That is not what grabs Annie's attention, and nor is it the gorgeous car. Annie stares at the man, shocked, because the driver looks remarkably like someone she knows.

'Hello?' says the Rake.

Annie is, for once in her life, speechless. 'I say? Are you deaf?'

Annie just stares at him. She knew he would speak like this, like all the posh people that came to The Hall for parties and suchlike. His voice is indeed very posh, but she can tell it has an Irish lilt. The Rake tries again. 'Excuse me … young lady?'

Annie smiles and her whole face lights up.

The Rake looks at Annie in a different way now. This is not just some local girl. This is a beautiful young woman.

'Ding dong!' the Rake says to himself, softly, about Annie's loveliness. And then, pulling himself together, he speaks to Annie.

'Do you live here?'

'When I'm not on the Riviera.'

'A wit too … Do you know Lady Helen?'

'I might,' says Annie, teasing. She's seen him look at her in that particular way, and she doesn't mind, not one iota. In fact, she loves the effect she has on men.

'You might? Hmm. I'll pay you but … it's our secret.' The Rake holds out a small package and a one pound note.

'Holy Mother of God!' says Annie at the sight of the note.

'Can you get this to Her Ladyship, without, I repeat, without anyone seeing?'

'Is the Pope a Catholic?' Annie tries to snatch the money. The Rake holds firm.

'My dad works here. I see Lady Helen every day.' Annie's begging now. She really wants the pound. 'Cross me bra and hope to die.'

'Our secret?'

'I swear!'

'Good girl.' The Rake lets go of the package, pushes his foot down hard on the accelerator and roars off with an impressive screech of tyres.

In the Montagues' bedroom at The Hall, Lady Helen peers out of the window towards the end of the avenue, which she can just see through the beech trees. She wonders who is being silly and showing off in some sports car.

Still standing right outside the main gates, Annie Cassidy stares happily down at the package and the pound note held firmly in her right hand. Annie opens the package.

She's in shock.

'Jesus, Mary and Joseph!' She is looking at a solid 24-carat gold, Art-deco, cigarette case. Engraved on the outside are three initials: H.D.M. She flicks it open. Inside, a yellow band holds five Sobranie Black Russian Cocktail cigarettes in place. There is an engraving; To Helen, love Bobby, April 10th 1944.

*

I walk into breakfast and I'm not going to be rattled as there's a small chance the old man may not have realized what time it is. I'll just be calm and it'll be fine. 'Morning, Dad.'

It doesn't work. Here we go.

'It'd be a damn sight better morning if you got here on time! Breakfast's at eight. You see your mother at 7.45 and come straight after. It's ten bloody past!'

Ah feck off.

'It's not my fault. I had to help the lads with the hay and ...'

'Don't apologize to me. Apologize to Bridget! We can't keep the staff waiting just for you.'

Stay cool now. Keep a sense of humour. 'Bridget? My sincere apologies.'

'That's all right, pet.' I keep my mouth shut for once as I know anything I say will wind him up but I'm still pissed off all the same, especially because of last night. So I go to the sideboard to check the breakfast and I can't believe it, there's no baked eggs, just fried. Feck! What the fuck is going on? Where are the baked bloody eggs?

Lucy puts me straight. 'Dur! Monday, poached with ham. Tuesday, boiled. Wednesday, kedgeree. Thursday, fried. Friday, baked. Get it?

'Get what?'

'It's Thursday, man. Come back tomorrow. Dig?'

'Oh yeah, I dig, *man*.'

'Cool.' I help myself to the fried eggs and then I take a couple of rashers of bacon. I check the old man's not looking and I wrap the rashers in a damask napkin and dry them. I hate the grease and I'm sure it makes me fat and spotty although Bridget says I look like a stick and if I turned sideways I'd disappear.

I'm trying to eat but it's hard. All I can hear is that fucker slurping and slobbering as he shovels porridge with lashings of cream into his big fat gob. His stupid dog, Cromwell, makes exactly the same sound sitting beside him.

Cromwell is a Rottweiler, or a butcher's dog as some people call them. Mum says the Nazis used them to guard the concentration camps. The old man loves Cromwell and Cromwell loves the old man, probably because the dog is always begging and the old man's always feeding him off his plate. Emma says only peasants do that, but the old man doesn't care, as Cromwell is the love of his life. Emma also says that Cromwell is a 'frightfully unwise name for a dog' because Oliver Cromwell was hated by the Irish for all the massacres he committed.

Anyway, there I am trying not to listen to all the slurping and slobbering, when I think it's time to have fun with my sisters. I whisper, 'Guess who else's been stuffing her face?'

The sisters look up, doubtful. Emma from her *Catholic Herald* and Lucy from *On the Road*, her trendy book, man.

'Oh yeah,' says Lucy, all sceptical. 'I don't believe you, man. No way.'

'Honest, *man*, she was. She had loads of orange juice with her vodka, and listen to this: she ate the whole cherry off the grapefruit. I'm not kidding.' Emma and Lucy laugh really loud and the old man looks up. He hates being left out of anything, especially a joke.

'What's so bloody funny?'

'She's lost her cigarette case,' I say, as quick as anything.

'Who's *'she'*? ... The cat's mother? Anyway, there's no point in asking you. You couldn't find your arsehole in a snowstorm.'

God, you think you're so bloody hilarious, you tosser. We all laugh just a little to humour him. Although we all, even Lucy, think he's vulgar.

Now the old man's all relaxed as he thinks he's made a terrific joke and he's wondering aloud to the world if he should get the vet to look at some stupid cow, number 33, that has sore teats and Emma all snotty says, 'Do you mind if we don't talk about cows' udders whilst I'm trying to eat my breakfast?' Bad move.

'Jesus Christ, if it wasn't for the cows, how else do you think this ...' he lifts a milk jug '... would get on your eff-ing cereal every morning?' I know it's a bad idea but I can't help it.

'From the milkman?'

Oh God, my big mouth. The old man's about to explode. I mean, stupid fucker, he thinks he's a farmer and he thinks that everyone thinks that he lives off the land and that he's not actually married to a rich woman and that he's the only person that ever got up to milk cows at five in the morning.

But instead of exploding, the old man gets really subtle and sticks the oar in. 'Have you told her?'

'Told who?'

'You know *very well who*. Your friend, Miss Annie Cas-sidy. About staying away from my house.'

'Tell her yourself, you big fecking bully!'

I storm out, slamming the door. Bridget calls our house 'The House of Slamming Doors'.

*

Bridget's mum, Mrs Collins, used to be in service herself and once told me that her last job was as housekeeper with a family who also slammed doors although they never had any children. This wild man, Black Bob Fetherstonhaugh, married a rich American lady who had bought a stud farm near Ballinasloe. Black Bob had lost all his inheritance play-ing cards and he only put up with his difficult wife because she held the purse strings. The Yank herself realized all along that Black Bob had only married her for the money and decided she was going to make the most of it. So she continued to give Black Bob a really hard time and bend his ear about everything.

One day while Mrs Collins was still there, Black Bob had decided he'd had enough and that the Yank he married for the money was 'no longer worth the hassle'. When he finally left his wife and her stud farm forever, he signed the visitors' book for the fifteen years they had spent together. He wrote, '*Thanks for the hospitality. Bob.*'

When I was very young and before I started riding race-horses I had a pony, the one that shat in the fridge. I loved Darkie but he was a terrible pain in the arse and would buck me off at the first chance he got and then he would stand there staring at me, all innocent. I rode Darkie to my first hunt, what they call a 'lawn meet'. The grown-ups were eating chicken vol-au-vents and knocking back bullshots served up by the maids. A bullshot was warm beef consommé soup with vodka added. It smelt great. They never got off their horses, the hunt followers. They just took the glass, knocked back the bullshot, and handed the empty vessel straight to the staff, usually expecting a second or even third sup. It was incredible that most of them managed to stay in the saddle all day after drinking so much.

I was only three years old but I wasn't scared as I was on a leading rein led by Danny on a much bigger animal. I do remember being embarrassed because Darkie wasn't clipped. He looked like one of The Beatles, just with longer hair. It was lucky we were on a lead, otherwise I think there was no way he could see through the fringe that covered his eyes and we'd probably have ended upside down in a ditch with him singing, '*Love, Love me do.*' I was ten when Darkie died. I'll never forget coming back from Dublin in the car and I could see way in the distance a tractor heading up the haggard with the front loader raised up high. On top was the limp body of poor old Darkie. I wanted to see where he was buried and say goodbye, but they wouldn't let me. The old man said it would be too upsetting. Years later Lucy told me he wasn't buried at all, that they fed him to the foxhounds at the hunt kennels.

The hunt kennels themselves were miles away but we used to go there when the old man had a few seasons as master of the hunt. The hunt was called the Kilcullen Harriers. Harriers are supposed to chase hares but our hunt didn't. It chased foxes. We could never change the name to the Kilcullen Foxhunt because then the hunt would be in real trouble. And this is the reason. All the area we hunted belonged to the Kildare Foxhunt. If the Kilcullen Harriers changed their name, they would be admitting that they were hunting foxes over an area where they weren't allowed to hunt anything but hares. So they just kept on hunting hares but chasing and killing foxes. By mistake, of course.

All the black and tan foxhounds were wild and stank like you would not believe, although they were friendly enough if you went up to them. Except for one hound. This hound was called Joker and it was a name that didn't suit him. Not at all. Joker was a really nasty bit of work. So whenever the hunt staff threw in a dead horse or an old cow for the hounds to gobble, they always put a special bit aside for Joker before the other hounds. Otherwise he would savage any hound that got near him. As Joker got older, his temper did not improve. If anything, it got worse.

One day there had been a hunt meet in Wexford and as usual at the end of a long hard wet day the forty hounds, steam rising, were loaded into their own transport, an old horsebox, to ferry them back to the kennels at Kilcullen.

When the hounds' box arrived, the hunt staff let down the ramp to let the hounds rush out and into their kennel for feeding. Imagine their surprise when they discovered that there were only thirty-nine hounds. So they checked the numbers again and again until the huntsman, knowing his hounds well, suddenly guessed what had happened. When they checked the box more thoroughly, they discovered bits and pieces, but not much else, of poor Joker's remains. On the way back from the meet, Joker had probably taken a lump out of another hound in a fit of pique and the others had decided that they'd had enough and his time had come.

Every year in April we had loads of guests for the Punchestown Festival, mostly relations from England. The festival itself is a fantastic five-day affair held in April and it is the only racecourse in Ireland where the horses have to jump stone walls and banks. Everyone from The Hall is invited to partake. There would always be two picnics: one for us and one for the staff. We would all go in the Jag and the Triumph and park up right next to the two or three staff vans. So the two picnics would happen right next to each other, parked right by the rails about one hundred yards past the winning post. A great spot.

A couple of years ago this one poor horse crashed straight into a fence in front of where we parked. It just ran straight into the fence at full pelt as though it wasn't there. It was a horrible accident but luckily the horse was killed stone-dead, so didn't suffer too much. And the inexperienced jockey was only slightly concussed.

When the horse's unfortunate trainer passed us, the old man offered his commiserations. The weird thing was, the trainer didn't seem too upset and even offered the dead horse as meat for the Kilcullen hounds, which was generous enough especially as he didn't hunt with us. The old man, having just become master of the hunt, accepted gratefully. The horse's body was transported that very afternoon to the kennels and was thrown to the hungry hounds who gobbled it up as fast as possible.

Within a few hours all the hounds were violently sick. Eventually most recovered but three died, including this huge black and tan hound that the old man had got from Dumfriesshire in Scotland. The hound's name was Mandrake and he was magnificent. Mandrake was a good few inches taller than the other black and tans and would lead the pack, sometimes running twenty or thirty feet in front. His cry, which was much louder and more piercing than the others, could send a shiver down your spine.

Sadly, it was obvious what had happened. For some reason the trainer had wanted his horse dead, insurance or betting or something. He had decided to drug the horse so that it would have an accident. No one could do anything about what had happened as by the time anyone had realized, all evidence had long gone.

Four

It is my rule never to lose my temper,
unless it would be detrimental to keep it.
Sean O'Casey

Thursday, 27 June 1963

I rush into the warm safety of the kitchen, slamming the door behind me. Emma and Lucy and me, we all come here when there's been trouble and we all stand by the Aga and have a good laugh with Bridget, and even Maureen Cassidy when she drops in for a cup of tea. And we try and forget them: the ructions. I look up at the wall and there they are, the two of them, side by side, just like in every house and shop in Ireland: JF bloody K and His Holiness, Pope John XXIII. Bridget says the fella who took these snaps must have made a fortune.

Paddy Kelly is sitting at the kitchen table wearing his dirty old tweed cap, supping his tea. Well, *slurping,* more like. Now I know why Paddy and the old man work so well together. They could *slurp* away all day at each other and neither of them would give a tinker's cuss about the disgusting sound.

Bridget is singing away to Paddy, all seductive and teasing as she brings him his bread and butter.

'*Are you lonesome tonight? Do you miss me tonight? Are you sorry we drifted apart?*'

Paddy's grinning and blushing like a right eejit and looking really embarrassed.

'*Does your memory stray to a bright sunny day when I kissed you and called you sweetheart?*'

I make a lunge for the bread bin and pull out the sliced pan. I grab a slice, smack it on the table to let Bridget know I'm upset, spread lashings of butter and then a delicious layer of sugar all over. I fold the bread and shove it in my gob, all crunchy and buttery and soft. Heaven! Now I feel better. 'Big fecking bollocks!' says I to the world, mumbling through the bread.

'Not Elvis, I hope,' says Bridget, quick as anything.

'Ah now don't worry the boss, me little gossoon,' says Cook, who hates any kind of ructions. Cook is so old and fat that all she can do is sit in the corner peeling potatoes. The only thing she can make is baked bloody eggs. Bridget swears Cook spends every holliers in the loony bin across the mountains at Newtownmountkennedy.

'Ahhhh, *don't worry the boss*,' says I, still annoyed.

'You are a bold boy, so you are,' says Cook, all indignant.

'*Paddy!*'

Oh fuck. The old man's standing at the door, red in the face, yelling. He's aiming at Paddy now, not me. Poor Paddy gets such a fright he drops the mug and spills the tea all over the floor. Bridget is not happy.

'Jesus, Mary and Joseph, boss! I'm only just after mopping it,' she says, furious.

This isn't the first time Bridget's had a go at the old man.

The old man has this thing about crows and he's always

opening the dining room window when he sees too many out on his lawn. 'Bugger off! Go on, get outta here! Get off my lawn!' he yells at the crows and they scatter, but to his fury they always come back to sit on his lovely mown grass.

One day, the old man's having his usual after-lunch siesta on a lovely lazy summer's day in their bedroom on the first floor. He can't sleep as he hears the bloody crows squawking away outside on his bloody lawn. 'Right,' he thinks. 'I'll get those noisy fuckers.' He gets off the bed and goes across the room on his hands and knees so that the crows, down below on the lawn, have no chance of seeing him. He sneaks like John bloody Wayne into his dressing room, takes his 12-bore Purdey shotgun, and comes back into the bedroom, still on hands and knees. He loads the gun as quickly as possible, pushes forward the safety catch, raises himself higher and aims through the window at the pesky crows. *'Bang!'* He lets rip with the first barrel, but gets a surprise. He's managed to shoot out all the glass on the window. The window was closed and he hadn't noticed.

At this terrible racket Bridget comes running out of the house and seeing what's happened lets rip herself, yelling up at the old man:

'Jesus, Mary and Joseph, boss! What the hell did you do that for? I'm only just after cleaning them windows.'

'Jesus Christ, Bridget. You might've bloody well told me!'

The old man is still furious and he's still standing there in the doorway of the kitchen, hands on hips, and now he's giving Paddy some serious jip.

'I thought you were supposed to be in the cowshed washing those heifers' tails, not lazing around in here, stuffing your face with my bread and tea.'

'Oh yeah. Oh yeah.' Paddy's muttering and rushing out

the door as fast as Ronnie Delany, Ireland's only Olympic gold medallist, ever. When you're a kid growing up in Ireland and you're seen running around the place like you do after drinking a bottle of Lucozade, the grown-ups love to shout, 'Oh God *look at him*. Just like Ronnie Delany.'

'Why don't you leave him alone?' says I to the old man. I'm still in fighting form.

'And you, you little bollocks. Stop hanging around in here, interfering with the work.'

'I'm not interfering!'

He's lowered his voice now and that means real trouble. 'Don't you backchat me.'

Bridget, aware of the danger, grabs me and shoves me out the door to safety.

'Oh God, Donal's forgotten the shopping list for Smith's. Come on, Justin. *Hurry!*'

We leave the old man fuming, hands still on hips but a little happier with the chaos he's managed to cause. We're moving down the back passage now to go and find Donal, and Bridget's trying to make me feel better. 'He's not that bad, really, your dad. He shouts and roars but then he forgets it in no time.'

'I don't.'

'I know pet, I know. It must be hard.'

I'm not thinking about the old man any more. I'm thinking about tea. How can anyone ever drink it? It smells like sick and the Irish think you don't need a doctor if you have tea.

'Oh Jaisus, I've broken me leg' … '*Ah, have a cup of tea.*'

'Me mother died' … '*Ah poor you. Have a cup of tea.*'

Bridget Collins, as I've already said, is brave as anything, especially with the old man. Bridget's been here since she was thirteen. Her dad owns a little farm in County Carlow and sometimes she invites me over at the weekend to spend a night with her parents when she gets a couple of days off, a very rare occasion. Once I walked into the staff room and caught her kissing Danny Keogh from the stables. Now I know what he was after. But then Bridget would never show her breasts to anyone, not till she's married. Not like the girl who was here a few years ago, Deirdre Mooney. Bridget once told me all the gossip about her.

Deirdre Mooney used to work in the laundry room, ironing and washing the sheets and all that. Deirdre had two problems – the bottle and the men, particularly the stable lads. As soon as she had a drink inside her, she would take one of the lads up to the hay shed and give them a good time. To give Deirdre her due, according to Bridget, she had a really wicked sense of humour even when it came to taking the mickey about herself.

Once in the middle of Bridget's first summer in 1955, when she had just started and I was four, Deirdre was helping Bridget to clean the windows of the loft at the top of our house where the indoor staff all slept. At one point a tractor and trailer go past way below, heading down the avenue, carrying a huge load of hay for the stables.

'Oh no. They're taking away me bed!' shouts Deirdre, all fake-sad and laughing at the same time. Poor old Bridget, who was young and innocent, didn't get the joke until a couple of years later after Deirdre was long gone, and Bridget was told the gossip by Danny Keogh about how Deirdre used to service all the lads in the hay.

Apparently Deirdre had another trick and it involved the old fire escape that led from my parents' bedroom down into the back yard. When the parentals were away and Deirdre had the job of cleaning the drawing room, she would take the opportunity to sample the drinks tray. In no time at all she would be scuttered drunk. Much the worse for wear, she would sneak up to my parents' room and onto the fire escape, where she would look out for the arrival of the farm hands who were coming in for their elevenses. Deirdre would wait until a whole gang of them were crossing the yard and would then rush out onto the top platform of the fire escape, turn around to face the house, bend over, hoist up her skirt and show the lads her arse. They loved it.

The old man finally had enough of Deirdre's shenanigans and she was asked to leave. Luckily her husband, Tony Mooney, had a good job with Kildare County Council so they didn't starve. In fact, at one point a few years later, Tony was made 'senior manager in charge of roads' and he started earning loads of money. So Deirdre, who was very house-proud, insisted that they build an inside bathroom, which not many people had in those days. This handsome young builder arrived, did a great job on the bathroom, and then an even better one on Deirdre, and she ran off with him. Poor old Tony was left with a large bill and a nice new bathroom, which was the envy of the neighbourhood.

Most people, according to Bridget, reckoned that Tony got the best deal in the end.

Five

Money does not make you happy, but it quiets the nerves.

Sean O'Casey

Thursday, 27 June 1963
Donal Sheridan, our chauffeur, stands by the car, which is immaculate as usual. The beautiful Mark II Jaguar is black, smart and gleaming with wax. It's lovely and it smells great inside, all red and leathery, but it's a little embarrassing as well. The old man's loud enough but so is the car. Whenever you drive anywhere, everyone stares. Nobody in Ireland has a car like this, only the president and the Guinness family.

Most of Mother's friends are posh but most of them, apart from the Guinnesses and a couple of other families, are poor. They live in big houses but there are holes in the roofs and they spend most of their time in one room because it's so cold they can't afford heating. If they have any spare money, they'll spend it on their horses. Even our house was freezing in the winter, so I always had a couple of hot-water bottles to take to bed. It was so cold sometimes that I would pass clean out on the tack-room floor after we had finished exercising the racehorses. The old man says it's because I am just 'a little weed' and that when I get a little older I should do what Black Bob used to do, 'sleep with the parlour-maids to keep warm'.

This one lady, who owned a hunt in the west, Baroness Molly Pakenham, couldn't afford to keep the hunt any more. So she disbanded it, sold the horses, but kept the foxhounds. Molly loved her hounds, all black and tans, and she let them live in her big cold Georgian house. Foxhounds are not like normal pets, they're wild, and they didn't really appreciate how lucky they were to live in such a posh house. So they just ate everything, including the sofas, and shat everywhere.

Anyway back to Donal our chauffeur, who is from Kerry, and does everything in slow motion. Donal is checking the shopping list for Smith's of the Green, the best delicatessen in Dublin. Bridget and I watch, trying hard to keep straight faces. Donal reads the list out loud, all slow in his Kerry drawl, very serious as always: 'Quails' eggs, beef bouillon, potted shrimps. *Potted* shrimps?' Donal is confused and looks to Bridget for help.

Bridget explains. 'Shrimps stuck in butter, Donal. That's all. And ...' Bridget gives me a wink on the sly and I know she's up to something, '... ten Carrolls please, pet?', handing him some coppers to buy her a packet of fags.

Bridget and I are trying hard not to laugh as we know exactly what Donal will give Bridget: a lecture. 'Now Bridget. I told you before, a packet of cigarettes is a brick for your house.'

'Yeah. Yeah. Thanks a million.' With a disapproving shake of his head Donal takes the money, gets in, and drives off. Well, moves off, incredibly slowly.

As the Jag disappears round the corner out of the courtyard and onto the avenue, Bridget and I do our act together. We both do great Kerry accents. '*A paaaacket of thigarettes is a brik fer yerr howss.*' We dissolve into laughter about how funny we are, and I think to myself how it's amazing that the old man, who is such a stickler for time, has a driver who is so slow.

One day last year Donal arrives back from posting the racing entries in Merrion Square in Dublin and he doesn't look well, like he'd seen a ghost. He says not a word to anyone and just walks straight in to see the boss man. The study door is closed, very firmly, and we're all hanging around outside to find out what terrible thing has occurred. After a couple of minutes there's a roar of laughter from the old man. Donal comes out of the study with a sheepish look on his face. It was the joke of the year: Donal Sheridan, the slowest driver in the whole of Ireland, had been caught speeding and had been given a ticket by the guards. He never lived it down. For Donal, it was the most humiliating incident of his whole life.

Donal was not only slow and serious but he was very religious and hated swearing of any sort. Even more than Emma, and that's saying something.

A few years ago the old man used to drink, but not like Mum, who is a slow and steady type of drinker. If he picked up a drink he would be gone for weeks. The weird thing was, he was much nicer with a drink inside him. It was only when he stopped that he would become peevish. Anyway, one time when he was in the middle of one his binges, he decided to go *on the batter* to Dublin. He swore blind to Mum that it was all innocent, that he had no intention of drinking and that he had some important business to carry out and a meeting with the bank manager.

Mum instructs Donal to drive the old man and tells him 'on pain of death, do not let Mr Montague out of your sight'. Donal took his duties very seriously, like everything else. So off they went to Dublin, Donal driving. A little while later when they were motoring round St Stephen's Green past the Russell Hotel, the old man tells Donal to stop, 'just for a minute', so he could pick up a parcel. Donal says he doesn't want to but the old man persuades him that he wouldn't be a second and that Donal should just 'keep the engine running'.

Ten minutes later, Donal, now a little concerned, goes into the hotel to discover that the old man has long gone. He has bolted through the kitchens. Donal was distraught as he didn't know how he would explain it to Mum.

Back at The Hall with Bridget watching from the sidelines, Donal was standing in front of Mum, cap in hand, mortified. Mum, furious, demanded to know why Donal had not done what he was told. Donal, bursting with indignation and fear of losing his job, couldn't contain himself. 'It's like this, m'lady. That Mr Montague, God forgive me, but he's only *a treacherous old fucker!*' Jesus, I wish I'd been there to see it. Mum for once did show some emotion. According to Bridget she nearly had a heart attack from laughing.

The Russell Hotel is a great place where we'd always go on a Friday, the shopping day. The old man would drive us all to town in the Jag while Donal would be off doing the actual shopping in the van. Before lunch, we'd spend a lot of time in the hotel bar, discussing which picture to go to in the afternoon. Mum would be knocking back the wine while we drank Pussyfoots. Pussyfoots were delicious. They were made of lime and lemon and grenadine and whisked up with the white of an egg. After the film decision was made, generally by the old man and always a cowboy film, we'd go to lunch.

On the way into the dining room there was a fish tank full of trout. If you wanted fish, you could choose your own trout and they would take it out, kill it, and cook it. That's what they told us. I'm bloody sure they never took a trout out of the tank. They had them all in the fridge. All the ones swimming around happily in the tank must have had a good old laugh at us for thinking they were going to be eaten. I'm sure I recognized the same ones time after time, and I'm certain I saw one give a sly old smile. I was a bit odd in my eating habits when I was smaller. I would start with tomato soup, then *oeufs Benedictine* (poached eggs, Hollandaise sauce, ham and a bun), and then tomato soup again for pudding. No one seemed to mind, especially the old man, who was always happy at the Russell. It was the only time he really relaxed, apart from on his boat.

The old man bought this lovely old yacht, the *Diana*, from some people in Scotland. She was all teak with beautiful lines; her hull was painted white and she had three masts with rusty red sails and was built in 1928 in the Firth of Forth. She weighed sixty-five tons, had a bathroom with a real bath, and even a couple of double beds. And right at the front in the galley there was an Aga stove with the pipe coming up through the teak deck. She was beautiful, really beautiful.

When we pulled into any harbour in Spain, France or even Portugal, everyone would come and look, even though there were much bigger yachts around, just because the *Diana* was so special. I didn't really like going on the yacht as the old man was always in such a bloody hurry, like: 'We must get to Brest by 18.00 hours. *No later!*' So I never had time to fish or do anything like that. Although one time we broke down in the middle of the Bay of Biscay – I was delighted, hauling mackerel over the side like there was no tomorrow.

My favourite time on the *Diana* was when the old man let me take the helm. Most of the steering was done from inside the wheelhouse but on a good day you could steer from behind on this little wooden seat. Sitting about ten feet up on a raised platform, I could look over the top of the wheelhouse and steer away, really feeling the movement of the boat, all seventy foot of it, as she rolled through the Irish Sea.

The *Diana* always had three crew. There was Billy Black, the deckhand who lived by the boat in Dunmore where she was kept. He would look after her and keep her all polished up and in working order. Billy had originally worked on trawlers but like most fishermen, he couldn't swim. Billy also had another problem – a strong weakness for the bottle. Sometimes when they were in some foreign port, Billy, scuttered drunk and very noisy, would row himself back to the *Diana* in the middle of the night singing, '*Fräulein, Fräulein*'. When I was much younger I always thought he was singing, '*Throw a line, throw a line*', which would have been much more suitable considering the circumstances. The two other crew were a cook, who we always got from an agency in Dublin, and an engineer. The cook always changed but the engineer was, more often than not, Liam Cassidy, who loved going to sea.

When Grandpa Charlton was alive, we used to spend time on his yacht, the *Sonic*. Now the *Sonic* was not little, not like the *Diana*. Grandpa would not be seen dead in such a small yacht: after all, the *Diana* was only seventy foot. So in 1948 Grandpa bought this beautiful motor-yacht, which had originally been built in 1930. He then spent £100,000 on the refit. The *Sonic* was about seventy yards long and weighed 280 tons. She had two huge funnels, a crew of thirty-three and a white ensign flying from the stern, which meant apparently that Grandpa was a member of The Royal Yacht Squadron.

This yacht was so big you could jump off the top deck into the water and really hurt yourself if you weren't careful. I loved her because there was loads of deck space to play on and a really friendly crew who made a fuss of me because I was the youngest. These holiday trips on the *Sonic* were always in August and either to the Mediterranean or to the west of Scotland. If it was to the Med, then the yacht would go out ahead of us and we would fly in our own chartered plane and meet her somewhere like Palma. We'd sail around the island, stopping off at beautiful old ports. During the day, the *Sonic* would drop anchor in these secluded bays with incredible clear blue water where you could see to the bottom, even though it was sometimes thirty or forty feet deep. We would jump off and go snorkelling.

When the chief steward, Mr Perkins, rang the bell for lunch, we would swim back as fast as we could and get on board in time to shower and put on our towelling dressing-gowns for lunch. These towelling robes were really comfortable and had *The Sonic RYS* written on the breast pockets in blue thread. The lunches themselves had weird food like *foie gras* and wild strawberries. I was shocked when I found out that the *foie gras* came from specially fattened goose livers, but I still ate it. If you are brought up on a farm you can eat anything. Much to my surprise, it was delicious.

Some days we would arrive in a port to be met by the harbour master all dressed up to the nines in his smart uniform, saluting our arrival. I think they thought Grandpa was pretty important. Out of nowhere a line of chauffeur-driven cars would appear and whisk us off to see some old village or monastery. But the best time for me was when we played games like badminton on the huge deck and everyone joined in.

If the trip was to Scotland, we would fly to London, then travel up on the sleeper train and meet the yacht in this little bay where Grandpa had rented a large castle for all his guests to come and stay for the grouse-shooting. The water was not as warm as the Med. It was bloody freezing. Every morning, Grandpa, standing on deck, all-important in his double-breasted blazer and captain's cap, would force us to parade in our bathing costumes and jump into the water before we had breakfast. God, it was cold. But I always felt better after a huge plate of scrambled eggs and devilled kidneys on toast.

When Grandpa Charlton died, Grandma sold the *Sonic* as she had too many fond memories of her. Not long after, the *Sonic* was bought by the president of some African country and hit a rock off the Canaries and sank. They said the captain was plastered.

Six

*The big difference between sex for money
and sex for free, is that sex for money usually costs a lot less.*

Brendan Behan

Thursday, 27 June 1963

*The gardens at The Hall are looking exquisite. Paddy Kelly
stands behind Liam Cassidy, who is on his knees in a flow-
erbed that runs down the side of a long rectangular lawn.
Liam is doing the real work, pulling the weeds and handing
them to Paddy, who is trying hard not to look at the boss
man watching, pipe in hand. Cromwell, by Bobby's side,
snarls at Paddy.*

'Well done, Liam. Ten times better.'

'Thanks, boss.'

'*Good man yerself, now!' Bobby adds enthusiastically
in his best Irish accent. 'Her Ladyship will love it.' Bobby
walks off with his beloved Cromwell.*

*Liam is relieved and congratulates Paddy who has done
very little but get in the way. 'Well done, Paddy. A grand
job. Really.'*

*Paddy is happy. 'Oh yeah, oh yeah,' he mutters. Paddy
worships Liam.*

*

I love lying here in the dusty yellow straw, hidden away between the bales. No one can find me in the hay shed, except Annie. I'm reading Mum's April copy of *Vogue* magazine. Not as sexy as *Playboy*, is *Vogue*, but this one model looks great in her Playtex underwear. 'Nice legs, baby,' says I. 'You're looking massive!' But of course if she's English she wouldn't understand.

Once my Aunt Daphne, Mum's second sister, who is 'fraghtfully English don't-ya-know', came to stay for the Dublin Horse Show in August. On the Saturday night she comes downstairs in her beautiful dress, all ready for the Meath Hunt Ball. Maureen Cassidy, thrilled, sees her and says: 'Oh my God, Lady Daphne. You're only looking massive!' Aunt Daphne was horrified at being called fat and immediately decided she was going to give up eating completely, until the old man pointed out that she was actually getting a compliment, not an insult. I'm not sure she ever believed him.

Anyway here I am in the hay shed, still waiting for Annie and gawping at the Playtex model who looks *massive* and I put my hands on my willy from outside my trousers of course, but suddenly there's a sound of rustling straw and singing: '*You would cry too if it happened to you, do do do, do do ...*' Annie's arrived. How come she's always happy? I wonder what it's like to be like that, always happy.

Annie, standing right over me, points an imaginary pistol and does her John Wayne impression, 'Okay pardner. Yer *Vogue* or yer life!' I hand over the magazine I've stolen from Mum.

'Sorry,' she says, 'I can't help it. It's all them cowboy films your daddy makes us watch.'

She starts singing again but I wish she'd shut the fuck up so I can tell her the bad news about not being allowed into the house anymore. *'For ever my darling, our love will be true ...* Especially if you keep fecking your mother's *Vogue.'*

Annie lies down all confident right across my lap and starts to read the magazine. I try hard not to get a stiffy by concentrating on something else, anything else. So I just rattle on.

'All the boys at school think *feck* means, you know, *fuck.* "Look," I said to them, "to *feck* something means to steal it." "So," they said, the English thickos, "so why do you say *feck* instead of *fuck*?" And I tried to explain it's more polite, but they didn't get it.'

'That's not their fault. I mean, between you and me, the Brits are a bit slow.'

'God, I hate it. Why can't I just go to school with you and the lads?'

'Ah, what the hell are you on about? A few more terms and you won't even talk to me. You'll be too busy, *canooood- ling with your chums.'* I hate this, her doing my voice, I really hate it and I'm still angry from before and I don't know how to tell her. Annie continues: *'Chums. I say, old chap, who's the girl? Oh no one really, old boy, just someone I knew vaguely, long ago.'*

'Oh shut the fuck up!'

'What?'

'Would you like it if I imitated you the whole time? Would you?'

'Jesus. I'm sorry. Honest, Justin. I thought you liked it.'

'I don't.' Now I feel even worse. 'Sorry.'

Annie is trying hard now to make conversation, to make everything better. She points to a photo of a beautiful model wearing a wedding dress. 'Oh, would you look at that?'

I can't think straight and I know I'll have to tell her and I'm ashamed. Annie notices.

'I'm really sorry, Justin. Honest.'

'No, it's fine.'

Annie quite rightly guesses it's something else. 'Oh Jaisus. He found out. The boss man?'

'About?'

'Me trying your mother's dresses when they went to the races?'

'No.'

'What then?'

I can't say it.

*

The gardens at The Hall are deserted. Liam and Paddy have left for lunch. Dressed in a navy-blue skirt, silk blouse and a light-yellow cashmere cardigan, Lady Helen Montague walks elegantly down the path where the weeding had taken place all morning. Helen stops, pulls out a packet of Sobranies, takes one and – click – lights it with her gold Cartier lighter. She looks at the packet of cigarettes. Blast, she says to herself, about the fact she does not have her gold case to put them in. Helen is annoyed about the case, not because it is beautiful, nor because it was a wedding present from her annoying husband, but because it's hers, and she hates losing things that belong to her.

As she strolls, she thinks back to what her husband was like before, when he was a real man. When Bobby asked her father for her hand in marriage, her father had refused, and Bobby let rip: 'Look, Lord Charlton, I don't give a tuppenny what you think. I'm not some snotty-nosed Old Etonian who's impressed by your title. I love Helen and I'm going to marry her. And if you don't want to pay for the wedding, that's fine. And if you cut Helen off without a penny and I have to marry her in a barn, that's fine too. We'll survive. So, put that in your pipe and smoke it!'

*

In the hay shed, Annie lies back in the straw, flabbergasted and upset by my news. 'Not allowed in your house? Jesus, Mary and Joseph. Why?'

'I don't know.'

Now she's staring at me with that serious look I love. 'Let's run away and get married.'

'Oh sure. Just like that.'

Annie's in dreamland. '… and we'll live on a farm by the ocean and I'll wear jewels and Sybill Connelly dresses just like your mam and everyone will know I've been past because of the gorgeous Chanel perfume I'm wearing.'

A shout from outside the hay shed ruins the moment. '*Annie?* Your dinner!' It's Maureen, Annie's mum. She always knows where we are.

'*Coming!* … But we can never be married,' says Annie, acting all sad.

I know we're not old enough, but I still feel disappointed. 'Oh. Why?'

''Cos you'll have to marry someone who has *lunch* and I'll have to marry someone who has *dinner*.'

'Eejit!'

She whacks me on the head with the magazine. 'See you later, alligator!'

I can't help smiling. She's happy at least. She's got her *Vogue*.

Once, when I was about six, this photographer arrived

61

from London. Mum had agreed to do a *Vogue* fashion shoot. Anyway, the photographer wanted a really wild shot of Ireland and the Wicklow Mountains with this beautiful aristocratic lady and nothing else to be seen but the gorgeous, untamed Irish landscape.

Everyone was away, and there was not one person to look after me. So Mum, to her great embarrassment, had to take me with these fancy fashion people on the shoot up into the mountains. I was, as usual, full of Lucozade and running around everywhere like Ronnie Delany. So to get me out of the way, she tells me to run down the road and back by the other road and complete a triangle of about half a mile. She promised to time me. Great. No problem. Off I ran, followed by this old lab we used to have. What she hadn't bargained for was how fast I was. I was back in a flash.

When the photographer arrived home in London and developed the prints, he discovered to his horror that the best photo he had was one with me running up in the background with the dog behind me. So much for gorgeous barren landscape with nothing else in sight. They published the magazine and there I was, tearing up the hill with Bran panting away behind me. There was an article about Mum and it even mentioned me and Bran. Mum was really annoyed for some reason. Lucy said it was because I had 'stolen her thunder'. But the funniest thing was that when I got to read the article, the bit where it says Mum's age had the numbers scribbled over so nobody could tell how old she was.

*

Lady Helen, walking through the garden, puffing on her Sobranie, is muttering to herself. 'Boring, boring. Bloody, fucking boring.'

As she reaches the immaculate Victorian greenhouses, she peers inside at the rows of white and black grapes hanging from the ceilings. Helen is not looking for something in particular. She is looking for some amusement to brighten her dull life. Helen leans down to stub out her cigarette on a neat pile of bricks, which are sitting by the greenhouse door. She has an idea. A sly smile comes to her face.

She picks up a brick, stands, looks around to make sure the coast is clear, then using the strength of all her frustration, smashes the brick through two different panes of glass. Slightly shocked by what she has done, she replaces the brick. Walking slowly back down the garden path and rubbing her hands together to brush off the earth, Helen's face appears to have changed. She is almost purring with happiness and whispers to herself: 'Not boring.' She sits down on a garden bench, enjoying her last smoke before lunch. She's in no hurry. She's used to people waiting for her. And, to top it all, she has, in one fell swoop, improved her morning. She's no longer bored and she's found a brilliant way to stir Bobby off his fat arse and into some kind of action.

At the Cassidy house, Delany, Annie's pet donkey, is tied up in the garden, chewing on an old Kellogg's Cornflakes carton. Still feeling raw after the news from Justin, Annie is too distracted to notice. She's staring at the package in her hand: 'So, you're going to banish me from your house, are ya, you miserable old fecker?' A determined look sets on her face. 'Deliver it, he told me. Deliver it, I will. Oh yes,' she promises herself. She doesn't quite know what the gold cigarette case is about, but she knows it could mean trouble at The Hall. That would be good.

Annie, clicking open the case, offers a cigarette to Delany in her best upper-class English accent: 'Hello, I'm Lady Helen. Do have one of my Russian cigarettes. Flown in from

Moscow. Wonderful, really, do, do, do!' Mulling over her magnificent plan, Annie walks into her house for dinner.

*

I'm on my way to the house for lunch, wondering what on earth Mum thought she was doing this morning, telling Joan she wants a reaction out of the old man. Jesus, that's the last thing we need. He's always bloody reacting. Anyway, she wants to be careful over the phone as the old man could be listening in downstairs in his study. And he wouldn't be the first person to listen in.

Our telephone number here at The Hall is Kilcullen 211. If we want to speak to someone, we have to wind the old phone a couple of times until it's answered by Mrs Lamb up at Lamb's, the pub. Mrs Lamb runs the local telephone exchange and the best pub around. Often she'd be pulling a pint for one of the lads and she'd hear the bell ringing and have to rush across the yard and answer the phone and put the call through. Mrs Lamb always swore blind she never listened in. But she did, for sure. Oh yes. Once Mum was chatting away with Joan, having a heated discussion about the day of the Beaumonts' party.

'It's on Friday,' says Mum, very sure of herself.

'No, no Helen, you're quite wrong. It's on Saturday. I'm absolutely certain,' says Joan.

'You're both wrong, m'lady,' pipes up the voice of Mrs Lamb from the exchange. 'I heard you discussing it with Mrs Beaumont herself. It's on Thursday after the Curragh races.'

Mrs Lamb was very useful at times. One night Mum wanted to speak to her good friend Beryl Mullins and asked Mrs Lamb to put her through. 'Oh there's no point in doing that,' says Mrs Lamb.

'Why's that?' asks Mum, all confused.

'The Mullins have gone to a birthday dinner with the Parnells. They're having venison and lemon meringue pie. I'll put you through if you like.' Mrs Lamb knew everything.

Although Mrs Lamb could manage the pub and the telephone exchange with great skill, she wasn't very bright. Years ago, when Aunt Daphne was staying, she asks Mum if she can use the phone. Mum, of course, says yes, but warns her to be careful of what she says, as Mrs Lamb is always listening in. So Aunt Daphne phones her dad in England. She tells Grandpa Charlton all about the old man's peculiar behaviour. Grandpa just loved hearing the stories about his strange son-in-law. He then asks Aunt Daphne to tell more but remembering Mum's words of warning, Daphne gets nervous. 'Actually Papa, I must be *frightfully* careful about what I say. Apparently the exchange lady always listens in.'

'I do not!' pipes up the indignant voice of Mrs Lamb, who hadn't missed a word of the conversation.

Grandpa Charlton had mixed feelings about my old man although all the cousins thought he was brilliant. To give the old man his due, he could be very funny at times, although not always on purpose. Uncle Freddie told me the great story of the old man's first disastrous attempt to ask Grandpa for Mum's hand. Everyone was staying at Charlton Park for a long weekend and all the younger relations suggested to the old man that the best time to get Grandpa in a good humour was after a big breakfast. So as soon as breakfast was over all the cousins, at a prearranged signal, snuck out of the room leaving him alone with Grandpa. Mum apparently was last to leave and she gives the old man a big smile and a flirty wink for good luck on the way out. As she goes out the door Grandpa looks up to find himself alone with the wild colonial boy. 'Yes? What do you want?'

The old man was, for once, at a loss for words.

'It's Helen …' he says, not sure what to say next.

'What about her?'

'… hasn't she got a great ass?' The old man had lost his nerve and just said the first thing that came into his head.

Charlton Park is like a palace, with thirty bedrooms and more than forty staff, indoor and outdoor. When you arrive in your car on this large area of crunchy gravel outside the house, you see huge steps and pillars, which are the main entrance, with the butler standing waiting. One time when Lucy arrived, a handsome footman was sent to carry her suitcase. Lucy was so busy ogling him she didn't notice her case was coming undone. It split open and all her clothes, including a large amount of knickers, fell back down the steps. I had never before seen Lucy so embarrassed or move so fast. It was hilarious. Of course if you were a grown-up, the staff would unpack the suitcases for you and at night-time, I swear to God, guests would go to their bedrooms after supper to find the toothpaste had already been put on their toothbrushes.

Another time we had all arrived for a long weekend and Granny didn't even know we were there until the next day. She only realized when she saw us all walk across the lawn past her morning room. Granny's butler, Wood, who had a terrible shaky head from some illness, had forgotten to tell Granny we'd arrived. When Granny knew we were all there, we would be summoned one by one for an audience after breakfast. Granny by this time was in a wheelchair. Wood would escort us individually into her morning room, which had these huge windows looking out onto the lawn. 'Master Justin, m'lady,' he would announce loudly. Granny would be writing at her desk and spin around with this big smile and put her arms out to give me a hug and ask me all the things I'd been doing. She was great, Granny was, and I miss her now she's dead.

One of the really fun things about Granny was her motorized wheelchair. It was custom-built by Bentley, the motorcar manufacturer, just for her. It had three wheels and a black leather cover, which you could pull up like a hood to stop the rain. Granny used to lend it to me and I would go whizzing through the formal gardens past the open-air opera house and the Victorian fire engine, which stood on display all proud and red in the Blue Pavilion at the end of the Long Pond. The pond itself was full of fish and had a huge fountain that you could turn on with a handle hidden in the water reeds.

There were two ghosts at Charlton: one 'inside' and one 'outside'. The outside ghost was a lady who used to be ferried around the gardens in her silver sedan chair. The inside ghost was a Cavalier, one of the king's followers from the Civil War, and he was very troubled, according to my Aunt Gwendoline, Mum's eldest sister. She told me that when she was my age, the Cavalier came to her and spoke. Gwen could see him in the long mirror in her bedroom and said that he didn't know where he was or even that he was dead. Gwen went immediately and told Granny. Granny, realizing that a Catholic priest was the only answer, waited until Grandpa Charlton had gone away on a business trip to South Africa. The minute he'd left, Granny called in a priest and the ghost was exorcised. Everyone in the family was sworn to secrecy as Grandpa would have had a fit about a Catholic, let alone a priest, being in his house.

Another great event at Charlton was the cinema evenings. The cinema was in the dungeon and had been a theatre for the house before films were invented. The cinema was full of wicker chairs and old French drawings and the staff would bring champagne and warm quails' eggs during the intermission. Granny always had the latest films sent down from London along with a whole film crew. (The projectors were already a permanent fixture in the next-door room, with their huge lenses poking through the wall.) But the film was always a surprise. We could never guess what it was going to be. For a laugh Uncle Freddie, when we asked him what it was going to be, would always answer, *The Ghost Goes West*. But it never was.

We could do anything we liked at Charlton and nobody ever shouted. The house was full of old pictures and old tapestries and old smells and I really liked this drum from the Civil War, which sat in the main hall. The hall itself had amazing wooden carvings by someone called Grinling Gibbons: pheasants and ducks and swans and fish as well as all other kinds of animals. The ceilings were incredibly high and there was a whole nursery wing just for us.

We used to get old Nursie, Mum's nanny, to read us *The Lion, the Witch and the Wardrobe*, although she was nearly a hundred by then. Nursie had this big mole on her face and she used to make us press it and she would go 'Buzzzzz', making a terrible sound just like a demented bell. It was really comical and we never got bored of pressing the mole. I bet she did. But she never complained.

Seven

*A man can be happy with any woman as
long as he does not love her.*

Brendan Behan

Thursday, 27 June 1963

It's lunchtime and there's terrible tension in the dining room. The old man, wearing a scowl that would frighten a hedgehog, drums the table with his podgy, hairy fingers. He's 'really vexed', as Bridget calls it. He checks his watch then drums the table again. Cromwell, that ugly Nazi camp guard, sits begging and dribbling beside him. The old man's hungry, Mum's late, and it'll be our fault if she doesn't hurry up. 'Where the hell is your mother? *The Lone Ranger*'s on at two. I'll probably miss it now!'

Asparagus tips a-bloody-gain. Bridget moves round the table pouring hot butter on the long green stalks that are supposed to make your wee smell. Come on Mum, *please!* As softly as possible I take the bottle of Lucozade and remove the crinkly yellow paper, pop the cork and pour a glass. The fizzing seems really loud, and I can feel the old man watching me. He stops tapping. 'Don't you ever drink anything else?'

Emma can't resist defending me by having a go at Mum's bad habits. 'It's better than getting plastered every day, isn't it?'

'Don't push your luck, young lady. You're skating on very thin ice.'

Lucy leaps to Emma's rescue. 'Dad? *The Lone Ranger*'s great! You really should've been a cowboy, don't you think?'

'Don't I know it. They've a good life, they have.' Now he's lost in his own world, thinking about being John Wayne come over to sort out the Irish.

So we're still waiting for Mum and the old man's looking tense again. For tense, nervous headache … take a Lucy Montague joke. 'Dad? What did the Lone Ranger say to his Indian when they got to the Canadian border?'

'Get on with it,' he says, only half-interested.

'Onto Toronto, pronto, Tonto!' The old man roars with laughter and the tension is gone just as Mum walks in clutching a bunch of flowers. Thank Heavens.

'Hello everyone. Lovely day.'

'Stand up for your mother. *Christ!*' We all stand without much enthusiasm.

'Sorry I'm late,' Mum says to the old man.

'Not at all,' says I to Mum. The sisters laugh.

'Not you, you twit! Bridget? Wine for Her Ladyship.' Mum sits, placing the flowers beside her. The old man doesn't notice and just starts eating like a wolfhound. Bridget pours the wine into Mum's glass, right to the brim, and then leaves. Mum, hardly eating, as usual, picks up the fresh-picked flowers and smells them, *sniffing* really loud. What the hell is she up to? The old man looks up like a perch at the bait. 'Good walk then?'

'Very pleasant, thank you, darling.' She sniffs again. 'Mmm, divine.'

'Well?'

'Excuse me?'

'Looks good, hey?'

'I'm a little lost,' says Mum.

'The garden of course!' He's looking for praise, that's what it is. And she knows it although she pretends she doesn't. So what's *she* looking for?

'The roses look amazing. Liam has olive fingers, not green,' says Mum.

The old man is thrilled. He grins like he's just won the Irish Hospital Sweepstakes. 'I told you he'd work well. Not easy to find someone like that. Lazy bloody Irish.'

'Just one thing …' says Mum. Uh ho. Here we go.

Suddenly she's changed her mind. 'No, no, don't worry. I'm being pernickety. Anyway, Justin? What have you been up to today?'

Is she pulling my bloody leg? Lucy and I look at each other. In all my years on this planet she's never asked me such a personal question.

'No, I insist,' the old man says to Mum.

'Oh well, if you insist …'

'I do.'

'I just think, occasionally, it might be a good idea to check the greenhouses. Seems to be a pane or two broken. That's all.'

The old man's livid. 'Jesus effing Christ!'

'Bobby? It's really not important.'

Now he's yelling at the door to the kitchen: 'Bridget? … *Bridget!*'

'Dad! Please!' Emma's trying to calm him whilst Mum sits there smirking.

Bridget pops her head round the door. 'Sir?'

'Liam and Paddy. Where are they?'

'At their dinner, boss.'

'Now don't be too hard, darling,' says Mum.

'You're too bloody soft! That's why I have to take charge. Bridget? You tell Liam and Paddy from me, they're to forget their effing dinner and go right now to the greenhouses and repair any panes broken. Tell them next time ... they're for the high jump!'

'Sir.'

'Jesus, you'd think they'd be grateful to have a job.'

Mum, of course, is delighted with herself. She swigs her wine and purrs. The old man as usual pets Cromwell because it makes him feel better. 'Good boy, Cromwell. Good boy!'

Christ. I hate the three of them. The old man, Mum, and that stupid German fucker.

I didn't always eat in the dining room. In fact, I'd only been allowed this great honour in the last year. The rule was that we ate in the nursery until we reached twelve years of age. The nursery was great fun at the beginning, with just Lucy and myself throwing food all over the place, but then I was alone for three years once Lucy had been elevated to the big league.

One time when I was just six, Lucy and I decided to have a midnight feast. During the day we managed to sneak all these goodies from the larder: quails' eggs, smoked salmon, potted shrimps, even Laura Secord chocolates from Canada that an old aunt used to send over every Christmas. There we were, Lucy and I, munching away on our delicious picnic by candlelight. It wasn't really that delicious and we weren't really that hungry. It was the illegality of the whole thing that made it exciting.

Suddenly there was an angry voice from outside the bedroom door. 'What *is* going on?' It was Mum and we thought we were in terrible trouble. But no, not at all. Mum admitted that she'd caught on to what we had been up to and she had decided to give us a surprise by bringing us extra goodies.

Well, she ruined the whole bloody thing, didn't she? To be fair to Mum it was really kind of her but she couldn't understand why we looked so disappointed. Then Mum didn't really understand children. Though I did feel bad for her afterwards. At least she tried.

*

Annie Cassidy, carrying the Rake's package, carefully opens the main door of The Hall. She's not quite sure what she is going to do, but in her own mind, whatever it is will be justified by the fact that she has never let people down, especially when she has made a promise.

Annie looks around the deserted entrance hall. She thinks back to the night before, when she saw that gorgeous creature, JFK, on the two tellies. Annie is distracted by a stunning display of red and white roses, which wouldn't be here if it weren't for her dad. She walks softly towards the silver bowl, reaches out, pulls a white rose down to her nose and inhales. She forgets all about why she is here, in Justin's house.

In the pantry, Bridget Collins, clutching a wet plate, stands frozen to the spot beside Mary, the new maid. Both are concentrating intently as President John F. Kennedy speaks to the Wexford people on the wireless:

'Mr Mayor, Mr Mayor, Chairman of the Council, Minister, my friends. I want to, er, I want to express, er, my pleasure at being back from whence I came. There is an impression in Washington that there are no Kennedys left in Ireland, that they are all in Washington. And, er, so I wonder if there are any, er, Kennedys in this audience, could you hold up your hands so I could see?'

Bridget and Mary immediately raise their hands. Bridget laughs: 'Ya little liar!'

'So're you!' says Mary, still laughing.

'Oh Jesus, the coffee! Quick, Mary, put the kettle on!' Mary rushes to the Aga, grabs the kettle, lifts a lid on the stove and slides the kettle across onto the hotplate. Bridget opens a cupboard in the pantry and takes out the Wedgwood coffee cups and saucers.

In the entrance hall, Annie clutches the silver-framed photograph of the Queen. Annie runs her hand across the glass, imagining what it would be like to go to Buckingham Palace and meet her. She notices a beautiful Chinese vase sitting above the fireplace. She replaces the framed photo carefully, then walks over to the fireplace, stretches up onto her tiptoes to reach the mantelpiece and takes a hold of a handle on the side of the vase.

'Hey!' Annie is taken by surprise, as she hears the boss man shouting, right behind her. She whips round but, at the same time, releases her grip on the vase, which falls to the ancient stone floor, smashing to bits.

*

The old man strides into the hall followed by Mum, Emma, Lucy and me, with Bridget behind carrying the coffee tray. Having heard the commotion I know something bad has happened. Jesus, Mary and Joseph! Annie? Am I seeing things? Fuck!

'What the *hell* do you think you're doing?' The old man, hands on his hips, glares at Annie. Silence. I can't speak and neither can Annie and I'm looking to Lucy to rescue Annie with one of her jokes. Quick, oh quick Lucy, anything please, just a quick one, like …

What does the American say to his wife at breakfast? 'Pass the honey, honey.'

What does the Englishman say to his wife at breakfast? *'Pass the sugar, sugar.'*

What does the Irishman say to his wife at breakfast? *'Pass the tea, bag!'*

Although to be honest we often tell these kind of jokes about Kerrymen instead of Irishmen because all the people where I live say that it's the Kerrymen that are the real thickos of Ireland. So it would be like …

Did you hear about the Kerryman who couldn't tell the difference between arson and incest? *He set fire to his sister!*

Back to the drama of the entrance hall and everyone's still in shock at seeing Annie and the smashed Chinese vase and I'm on my knees helping to pick up the pieces and whispering to her, to Annie, 'Are you crazy?'

But before she has time to answer the old man repeats himself: 'I said, what the *hell* do you think you're doing?'

Good old Emma's in there, quick as a flash: 'She's looking for me.'

'What?' says the old man, all confused.

'I am,' says Annie, all innocent with her big eyes wide.

'Why?' asks the old man, all suspicious.

'Mind your own bees' wax! Girls' talk,' says Emma, fronty as anything. She grabs Annie and strides towards the front door. 'Where were you? You were supposed to be here an hour ago.'

'Sorry, I forgot. But what about the vase?' asks Annie. Oh just go Annie, run, for fuck's sake, while you still can. Run like Ronnie Delany.

Luckily, Bridget's on the ball. 'I'll clean up. That's my job, not yours.'

The front door slams as it always does in our house. Emma and Annie are gone and I'm breathing a deep sigh of relief, but why do I bother? I know what's coming. 'You! My study. *Now!*' Oh shit! Now I'm for it.

*

In the gardens, Emma Montague strides purposefully along. Annie follows gratefully. 'Thanks a million, Emma, really.'

'What were you doing?'

'Looking for Justin.'

Emma stops, a little put out that Annie thinks she's so gullible. She offers Annie her crucifix. 'Hold this and tell me again.'

'I can't say. I promised ... hi Dad!'

Liam is replacing the broken glass at the greenhouses. He hasn't the faintest which child could have done such a horrible thing, but he's not going to let it spoil his day. 'How are ya pet? Emma? How's it going?'

'Fine thanks, Liam.' As they continue to walk, Emma pushes Annie. 'I'm waiting.'

'A man, a gentleman, asked me to give a message to your mother, in secret.'

'What message?'

Annie hesitates.

'I said, what message?'

Annie hands over the Rake's package. Emma opens it and recognizes the cigarette case. She realizes what has happened.

'Am I in trouble?' asks Annie.

'No, Dad is. Please Annie, tell no one. Especially Justin.'

Back at The Hall, in the comfort of his study and where he most feels like a man, Bobby sits, picks up a pipe and lights it. Puffing smoke he reaches for his coffee, slurps loudly and settles back into his favourite armchair. The Lone

Ranger *theme song begins: 'The Lone Ranger! Hi Yoooo Silver!' Bobby cannot relax. He hates the anger he has inside, and he hates the boy. He knows, logically, that it's not the boy's fault. But he cannot help it, this anger, and he just wants to rip Justin's head off every time he sees his horrible little face. And, Bobby reasons, why the fuck should I have to suffer the humility of pretending he is my son when he doesn't even look like me?*

*

I'm standing at the open study door waiting for my execution. 'Shut-the-door-sit-down-shut-up!'

'You said you wanted to see me.'

'After. *Sit!*' Oh great. Now I have to wait for the bloody Lone Ranger. I sit down on the foot stool in front of the old man and try to concentrate on the tellies. Bloody cowboys. Now I'm staring out the window, trying to forget. There's old Sean Plant with the lawnmower, trying to get it started. I hope it takes off on him and I hope he gets pulled into the bloody ha-ha and lands up in the nettles. I did that once as a kid in my bathing suit. I was stinging for ages and the dock leaves didn't help. Suddenly the Lone Ranger appears on his stupid white horse. '*A fiery horse with the speed of light, a cloud of dust and a hearty Hi Yo Silver! The Lone Ranger. Hi Yo Silver, awayyy!*'

I can't stop fidgeting, I know it'll annoy him but I just can't help it and I feel like being sick and it's not just the whole bottle of Lucozade I drank. Now I'm blocking his view.

'*Shift!* To the left.' So I move to the left but his eyes are still drilling holes into the back of my head. I try again to concentrate. Christ, and people are surprised when I say I don't like cowboys. '*With his faithful Indian companion,*

Tonto, *the daring and resourceful masked rider of the plains led the fight for law and order in the early west.*'

He's had enough, with me fidgeting away like a flibberti-gibbet. 'Right!' He jumps up and strides to the telly, the one with the blanket covering it. '*Return with us now to those thrilling days of yesteryear. The Lone Range ...*' He switches off the sound.

Now he's facing me like his cowboy hero, legs apart, and pointing the sucking end of his pipe in my direction, spitting out bits of Peterson's Old Dublin Tobacco, all sweet and disgusting. Peasant.

'I've had the last straw with that hussy. You will not only not have her in this house, you will not see her again. End of story!'

'You're pulling my leg?'

'Whilst you live under my roof, you will do as I say. Understood?'

'It's Mother's roof, not yours.'

His face drops. Got you, you cunt!

'You cheeky fucker! And you're hers, not mine,' he says, quick as a flash.

Now he's got me. 'What? What do you mean?'

The old man hesitates, thinks hard for a while. 'Nothing,' he says. 'You're your mother's special boy, aren't you?'

'You could have fooled me.'

'Let me put it this way, Sonny Jim. I don't want to have to sack Liam Cassidy because of you.'

Annie's dad? I can't believe it. Surely not. He's not that cruel.

'You heard.'

Now I've lost it and all the anger I've been holding in for years comes flying out and before I know it I've forgotten all the tricks I learnt at the Kilcullen Boxing Club and I am charging straight at him, right for his bollocks, yelling my lungs out, 'Ahhhhhhh!'

'Oi!' The old man's stunned for a second as I hit him hard in the balls. In a flash, he grabs me by the throat, shoves me against the wall and draws his huge hairy fist back, ready to punch. I'm delighted, thrilled, because then the whole world will know what a fucking animal he is by the bruises and the broken nose and teeth and black eyes.

Knock, knock!

The old man lets me go, a look of shock on his face. He can hardly move with fright, so I move myself very bloody fast and shove his fat fingers away from my throat and step back.

'Come, come in,' he says, trying to sound pipe-smoking calm but all shaky and clearing his throat.

Bridget pops her head in. 'Boss? The new priest has arrived. Father Luke.' I'm out the door in two seconds flat with Bridget following. In the hall is the new priest, Father Luke, waiting in a chair. He's trying to look all relaxed and casual but he can't be, not really. He must have heard about the old man. He's probably terrified. 'He'll see you now, Father,' says Bridget.

Father Luke leaps up all polite, too polite. 'I'm so sorry, young man. Did I interrupt something?'

'Yeah, actually. That fecker was just about to beat the living daylights out of me.'

'I beg your pardon?'

'Pay no attention, Father,' says Bridget. 'What a family. Always a banter!'

'I'm not joking, Bridget. He'd have killed me if you hadn't interrupted.'

'Ah now, don't exaggerate, pet.'

'I'm not exaggerating, you stupid bitch!'

'Justin?' I'm off down the passage like a scalded cat with

Bridget's worried shout chasing behind me: *'Justin?* Come back here. *Justin!'*

The gun room's not locked. Inside it's full of dead foxes' masks, boxes of Eley cartridges, rows of gumboots, hunting crops and a gun case lined with green baize. Inside the case are four shotguns: a pair of the old man's, one for Lucy and one for me. Still panting away with almost enjoyable anger, I remove my shotgun: the 20-bore Holland and Holland. Next, I grab a bandolier of ammo, throw it over my shoulder like Pancho Villa the Mexican bandit, and rush out, and I'm moving a lot faster than Mr John Bloody Wayne. I'll fucking kill him. I want revenge and I want it now.

*

In the study, Cromwell watches with interest as Bobby Montague, trying to pull himself together, delivers the new priest his instructions. Bobby finds these types of meetings a pain. Why could the old priest, Father Flash, not have done his bloody handover properly and just told the man how to behave? It would save so much time and trouble.

'Right, Father, down to business! If you have any problems, financial or otherwise, our door is always open.'

'Thanks a million.'

'A tree-planting, a case of claret, a spot of hunting for yourself. You do ride, of course?'

'No, I don't, I don't really believe in ...'

'Never mind that! Anyway, even a new roof, I'm your man. The door is open as I ...'

'That's wonderful.'

'I haven't finished.' Bobby does not like being interrupted by lesser mortals. *'I have only one rule. Mass will not last longer than thirty minutes.'*

Father Luke is rocked. He cannot believe what he is hearing and starts to protest: 'Begging your pardon, Bobby ...'

'Bobby, is it? If you don't mind, I'm not missing The Lone Ranger *and it's already started. See you Sunday, Father.' Bobby holds the door open, inviting the priest to leave, but the Rottweiler flies out instead. 'Oi, come back! Cromwell! Come back. Jesus bloody Christ!'*

The new priest is speechless. None of his training in the Mullingar seminary had prepared him for an encounter like this.

*

Up across the yard and I'll have to tell Annie the terrible news and then I'll go up into the woods where I'll have to kill something or I'll probably kill the old man as the pressure's just too much. Suddenly I hear something behind me. 'Ruff ruff!' Oh no, that bloody mongrel is following me. Cromwell loves shooting but I normally remember to make sure he's locked up so he can't follow. Cromwell is not a gun dog, he's a bloody nuisance, and he'll just rush around frightening everything before I have a chance to fire.

'Get lost! *Home!*' But Cromwell flies past me and I know there's nothing I can do. 'Heel, you fucking mongrel. *Heel!*'

*

Father Luke cycles back up the avenue towards the main gates. His hands are sweating and slipping round the rubber handlebars. He fails to engage third gear and bashes his knee in the process. He cannot believe what has happened. As far as Luke knew from what he had been told by the older priests in Mullingar, he, like every other priest in Ireland, would rule the roost in his new parish. He had been assured that he would be able to tell his new parishioners how to behave, and he had been really, really looking forward to going to the local dances and making sure that unmarried couples did not get too close on the dance floor. Luke cycles faster and faster as he rides out through the main gate of The Hall and up towards his church.

Eight

Every action of our lives touches on some
chord that will vibrate into eternity.
Sean O'Casey

Thursday, 27 June 1963
I'm outside the Cassidys' house with Annie and I've told her quietly, in her front garden, what the old man has said. I told her not to worry, that we'll meet on the sly, but that it's real important everyone believes we're sticking by the rules, even her parents. Annie shouts at me very realistically as I leave her garden. 'So? You just give up, just like that?' Good girl!

'Annie? Annie! Come back inside, this instant!' shouts her mother.

'Sorry, Annie, sorry.' I slink away, head down.

'*Ya little coward!*' screams Annie. What an actress.

*

In the Cassidys' front room, sitting round the wooden kitchen table, Liam and Maureen watch Annie, concerned. Annie cannot hide her feelings from her parents and as much as she admires Justin's bravery, she doesn't really believe he has a hope in hell of winning any battle against his father.

'He can't do it, it's not fair, he can't!'

'He can, and he has,' says Liam, firmly.

'He's just a big fecking bully! This is the Sixties, not the Twenties. And I'm not staff.'

'She has a point now, Liam,' says her mother, kindly.

'Maureen ... Jesus, Mary and Joseph, you're not helping. Annie, please – you'll just have to make another friend. That's all there is to it.'

'Am I not good enough?'

'You know you are, love,' says Maureen. 'But your dad's got a point now. People from Justin's background move in a different world. They're like people from another planet, and they'll never accept you, not in the way they should, anyway. Sad as it is, in no time at all you'll be like strangers, you and Justin. That's God's own truth.'

'Never, ever, ever!' says Annie, not really wanting to believe something she had always known to be true.

'And I cannot afford to lose my job,' says Liam. 'If you don't believe me, look at the dole queue next time you pass. See how long it is. And where do you think we'd live if that happened? This is not our house.'

'Why does God let the sun shine on some people and not on others?'

'Well, pet,' says Liam. 'Why don't you just swap places with Justin then?'

*

I'm stalking through the trees and some fucking pigeon is going to get it *right up its hole*.

Suddenly that stupid fecker Cromwell gallops ahead, barking away, scaring the birds who fly out of the trees at a hundred miles an hour in all directions. '*Idiot!*' I scream.

So, fast as lightning I put the gun to my shoulder and I fire twice at a distant and disappearing bird and ... nothing. I missed by a bloody mile. Bugger! 'Here Cromwell. Here, *come here*!' I slump down on some soft old moss under the big oak tree on the edge of the forest and wait for the birds to return. Then I'll get them, but I'm just boiling inside. Fucking pigeons.

Cromwell sits opposite, keeping his distance. He's staring at me all worried as he knows anger when he sees it. He's got that look that says, 'Please, *please* say something nice and I'll come and lick you all over and I'm sorry, I really am sorry, honest.'

'Shit!' I'm still thinking about the old man and I pick up some dirt and throw it at that fecking mongrel. But now he's growling at me. Whoops, careful Justin. Don't push your luck. He's Gestapo after all. Hold on, hold on, I've got it. I've had a brainwave. I know how to get my revenge. I know *exactly*.

I grab the Holland and Holland, break it open and the two used cartridges fly out *pop, pop*, onto the grass. I pick up one used Eley 7-gauge cartridge and smell it. Lovely, that smell of cordite. I grab two fresh cartridges from my bandolier and slip them into the gun, all the time grinning at Cromwell with delight at what I'm about to do. I close the gun, *clunk*, push forward the safety catch, *click,* and put the gun to my shoulder and tuck it in, all snug-like. I raise the 20-bore all slow and now I can see right down the barrel, past the gunsight, straight at Cromwell. And the best bit? He's staring at me all quizzical, with his head to one side, like he's asking what I'm doing. You'll soon find out, boyo.

*

Back at the kitchen table, Maureen rattles on with her memories. 'I remember when he was born, Justin. A squashed tomato, that's what he looked like. I mean, God, I'd never seen a baby before, although I was pregnant myself, of course. Her Ladyship was very kind and invited me up to see him. The Queen's nurse came over, Nurse Rowe from London, and she stayed three weeks. The girls themselves used to come over and see me when they were small, too. Emma was always quiet, but Lucy always wanted to know everything, why you do this and why you do that ...'

Slam! The door shuts and Annie disappears. Maureen looks up, surprised. 'Holy Mother of God! Where's she gone now?' Maureen jumps up out of her chair, but before she can go anywhere, Liam takes her arm and sits her back down.

'Leave her be, pet. Leave her be.'

Out in the garden, Annie hugs Delany for comfort. Delany keeps chewing. Bang! Bang! Two gunshots go off, way in the distance. Annie smiles to herself, thinking how funny it is that the boss man relieves his anger by bullying Paddy, and that Justin relieves his by shooting birds.

*

I feel better now, a whole lot better, as I walk into the entrance hall carrying the leather gun case and an old newspaper. I open the case on the hall table, remove the cleaning rods, the bristle brush and a tiny wool mop and the oil, and I lay everything neatly on the newspaper. I pick up the gun and break it into various sections. I'm thinking about Charlton, where the butler always ironed *The Daily Telegraph* before anyone read it so that we wouldn't get ink on our fingers. Now I'm thinking of the old man's strange habit of leaving typed notes everywhere.

One summer's morning I went to the fridge and there was one of his messages sellotaped to the door:

'*If you let a fly in, please let him out again!*'

Our area is full of flies, especially in a hot summer. This was partly because we had so many animals, especially the horrible Friesian cows who are always splattering their shitty pats everywhere. Obviously he'd opened the fridge door one day and a fly had flown out. But to leave a note about it seemed to me to be a little bloody weird, even for him.

'Hey Justin, old cock?' He's leaning over the stairs looking down, speaking all cheery. Good. He's obviously feeling guilty and so he bloody well should. 'How did it go? Get anything? Another left and right?'

'Cromwell messed it up by running all over, scaring the pigeons.'

'Sorry about that. He just ran out before I could catch him.' All right, enough of the polite stuff. I can't get used to it. Let me get on with my cleaning.

'Anyway, where is he?' asks the old man. I keep cleaning the gun without looking up. Fuck him. I'm not going to answer.

'Am I talking to a wall? *Where's my effing dog?*'

'I shot him.'

'Don't smart-arse me.'

I go to the pantry door open it and yell. 'Cromwell? *Here,* you big German lout. Your lord and master awaits you.' Cromwell comes flying through the door and up to the old man who bends down to meet the love of his life, all because I didn't have the guts to pull the fecking trigger. Now Cromwell is kissing him on the lips. I mean, the dog licks his own arse and even his bollocks and then he licks the old man on the face. Yuck. 'He could be carrying all kinds,' says I, thoroughly disgusted. Ignoring my health warning, he walks off with his mongrel but can't resist another attempt at being friendly.

'Oh by the by, I sorted the new priest. We should have no problems on Sunday. Hah!'

'*Hah*,' says I, and make a V-sign at his hairy departing back.

We're going to miss Father Flash, our old priest. He was 'a gas man' as they say, and apparently quite serious when he first arrived. But he mellowed over the years. Before he came to our parish, Flash used to be based in the west of Ireland and once told me a great story about his Saturday confession. This one farmer, Mick, had been hanging around the confessional for a couple of Saturdays, but had shown no interest whatsoever in entering the box to confess his sins. This confused Father Flash, who decided to confront him. 'Michael Healy? You've been lurking around my confessional every Saturday for three whole weeks and you haven't so much as poked your head inside. What are you up to, Michael? I want the truth now, boy.'

'Well now, Father, the truth it is you want? I'm waiting to hear who stole my effing load of hay. That's the truth.' Someone had fecked a load of hay from Mick's farm and Mick was convinced that if he hung around long enough he would eventually hear the culprit confess.

Father Flash was very fond of hunting and even owned a racehorse that the old man had given him. The horse was called Slow Melody and that's exactly what he was, slow. To be fair he wasn't that slow. He just didn't like racing. In a fit of pique, the old man had decided he was going to send Slow Melody to be eaten by the hounds of the Kilcullen Harriers as he would never win a race. But Father Flash had a soft spot for the horse and asked if he could keep him as a hunter.

The old man, mystified, demanded to know where Flash

was going to keep Slow Melody. 'I don't want to see that bloody animal anywhere near my fields. All he does is remind me of all the money I wasted trying to get him to actually win a race.'

'The Good Lord will provide,' answers Flash. And he did. For the want of a field, Father Flash kept the horse in the graveyard where there was plenty of lush green grass between the graves. And the funniest thing was, Slow Melody took to hunting like a duck to water. Father Flash became the envy of the Kilcullen Harriers as he tore across the countryside at full pelt.

The old man just loved being Master of the Kilcullen Harriers because it meant he was in charge and could feel really important and boss everyone around. But one day he got his comeuppance. A while ago we had a man working at home, called Brendan Plant. Now Brendan was a superb rider and could even, according to all the lads, have made the Irish team for three-day eventing if he hadn't had such a drink problem. Brendan was once in terrible trouble for missing a day's work. He was somewhere in Dublin, scuttered drunk, and unable to get home. So he was fined a week's wages and just had to accept it as there weren't any other jobs around, especially for a drunk. But Brendan didn't forget.

About a week later there was the opening meet of the hunt season. For some reason the Duke, the old man's hunter (named after John Wayne, surprise, surprise) was very fresh and lepping around the place. This was the start of the season and of course he was going to be fresh. But the Duke was more than just fresh. He looked totally wild and I am sure it had something to do with Brendan as he was the only person at the whole meet who didn't look startled.

Now the old man would never back down as pride was at stake, but when we started jog-trotting along the road to the first covert, the Duke was out of control, jumping all over the place and lashing out at everything in his path. The old man was shouting out to anyone who got in the Duke's way: 'Make way for the Master! Make way for the Master!' He was trying to pretend to everyone that he was in control.

The huntsman started away drawing the first covert and soon the hounds gave voice. Having picked up a fox's scent, we were off, tearing across the Kildare countryside with its stone walls and huge double banks. Suddenly we were all stuck in one field, gawping at this huge ditch. Jumping into a field is one thing but jumping up and out, is another. After all, ditches were built to keep the cattle from escaping.

At this stage the black and tans, led by Mandrake, were way ahead, running up a steep hill in full cry and there was a danger we would lose sight of them. I don't think I had ever seen a ditch as big and my pony wanted nothing to do with it, which was a great relief for me, I can tell you. As we waited for the huntsman, Jack, to find a way across, the old man suddenly appears and his face practically changes colour at the obstacle in front of him. Brendan was watching with delight: his moment had come.

'Make way for the master!' yells Brendan as loud as possible. 'Make way for the master, *please*!' As all eyes were now on him, the old man had no choice but to have a go, and he and the Duke landed upside down in the ditch in a big heap. Luckily for the old man it had been raining and so he just sunk further and further into the mud as the Duke lay on top of him. It was hilarious.

Jack was really small and looked like a fox. He drank like a fish and because he needed a tipple before the off, we often wouldn't get started until at least one in the afternoon, which didn't leave much time until dark. However, Jack generally only did this when there was a full moon as he could then hunt on into the night. It was really wild and dreamy, hunting by the moon.

Our first hunt of the season would usually be in Kildare, at a famous pub called The Hideout, in a village called Kilcullen. I love The Hideout for one reason. It has Dan Donnelly's right arm displayed in a glass case. Donnelly was a famous Irish boxer who managed to beat all the English and become a national hero. I could sip tomato juice and stare at the bones of his arm for ages. You wouldn't believe how long it was. If you ever look at the paintings of Donnelly, you can see his arms stretching right down past his knees. And if you ever go to the Curragh you can see a monument at Donnelly's Hollow where he fought a famous victory, beating a brilliant English boxer, Tom Cooper, by breaking his jaw.

Nine

He was born an Englishman, and remained one for years.

Brendan Behan

Sunday, 30 June 1963

I'm late for Mass, on purpose, and Mum's giving me a lift as she's on her way to Church herself. Mum goes to the Protestant church a little way up in the mountains by a beautiful rocky stream. As a child I used to play there when she was busy doing flower arrangements with Canon Winterburn. What a beautiful place, all those clear pools of water, miniature mossy swimming holes running down past the tree-shaded church.

I remember this one time when we were staying with Granny at Charlton Park. It was a beautiful sunny day and lunch was laid out outside on the loggia. We were surrounded, as usual, by maids and footmen wearing frock coats with big shiny brass buttons. Granny was sitting at the head of the huge long polished table and she says to us, Emma, Lucy and me, 'Now children, there's chicken or fish or lamb or kidneys or whatever you want.' And she points at all the different dishes on display.

'No, there's bloody not!' interrupts the old man. 'This is

Friday, Lady Charlton, and they're having fish, nothing else. You're not making bloody Protestants out of my children, thank you very much.' Granny laughed. She thought it was really funny. So we ate the fish and remained Catholic.

So back to Sunday morning and Father Luke's first Mass and I arrive at our church in Mum's flashy black Triumph Spitfire Mark 1 and there're no people outside, just a few old cars and tractors and bicycles and our beautiful black gleaming Jaguar. 'Thanks *Mother!*' I shout and she's gone in an angry cloud of dust, about being called *Mother*. I can't help it. Anyway what's she complaining about? It's better than putting bangers in her cigarettes, which I do when she's really tanked up. That she hates.

You can buy them in Dublin, these bangers. They're little rectangular pieces of cardboard about the same shape and size as a nail file. You just slip the dangerous end into the top of the cigarette. It goes in very easily and disappears between the cigarette paper and the tobacco. As soon as the victim lights up they will manage just three or four puffs and then *bang!* The cigarette explodes and the smoker is left shocked and then livid.

I look around, the coast's clear, as everyone's in Church. I sneak quickly up to the Jaguar keeping low just like James Bond. I have a spare set of keys in my pocket and I unlock and open the passenger door. Fast as anything I lean across the red leather seat and flip down the glove compartment. Inside is a wad of cash. He'll never notice a bit missing. Just as I stretch across and grab it there's a low snarl from behind me. Oh, Holy Mother of God! That fecking killing machine of a Nazi is sitting on the back seat protecting his master's car and now he's lunging for me. I drop the money and jump out quick as anything. *Slam!* I shut the door. Breathing fast with fright and because I'm running out of time I have yet another sudden brainwave. The old man was wrong. I'm not stupid. I'm a genius.

I have a few sugar cubes in my pocket that I keep for the horses. I hold out a lump at the snarling Cromwell through the closed window. Cromwell stops snarling and looks interested. I open the door real careful, smiling, offering the sugar and comforting words. 'Good boy, Cromwell. Yes, yes. Sugar. What a lovely ugly fucker you are.' Cromwell, thrilled with himself, snaps the sugar lumps off my hand and starts munching. Delighted and relieved, I snatch half the money, replace the wad in the glove compartment, jump out, slam the door and lock it. Time for Mass. But not before I've finished with that Nazi mongrel. So I stick my face against Cromwell's window, squashing it and making a horrible sound. Cromwell goes apeshit, snarling and barking and slobbering and baring his teeth as he bangs his head trying to jump through the closed window to get at me.

*

St Mark's church is packed to the rafters. The women, as always, are sitting on the left, and the men on the right. Many of the children are wearing gumboots. One child is even barefoot. Handsomely dressed compared to the impoverished locals, Bobby, Emma and Lucy Montague sit in the front right pew. No one else would ever dare sit there. A few rows behind on the left, Annie Cassidy sits with her mother.

Annie stares with hatred at Bobby's back. She imagines herself walking up to Bobby and saying something really horrible in front of all those people, to make him look like a complete eejit. But then she remembers her dad and his job.

Everyone stands as Father Luke, very determined not to be bullied, walks noticeably slowly into the church, followed by two altar boys who wear football boots peeping out from under their cassocks.

'Where's your brother?' asks Bobby, whispering as quietly as he is capable of to Lucy. Lucy shrugs her shoulders. No idea.

Father Luke begins.

'For those you of who do not already know, you have a new parish priest. I am Father Luke Conlon. I am so glad to see all of you here on my first Sunday in charge.'

'In charge?' says Bobby to his daughters. 'My arse!' Lucy stifles a laugh. Emma looks disapproving.

Father Luke starts the service, very slowly: 'In the name of the Father, the Son and of the Holy Ghost.'

The congregation snaps back.

'Amen!'

Father Luke is taken aback but quickly regains his composure.

'My brothers and sisters, to prepare ourselves to celebrate ...' Luke hesitates and stares down the aisle at the young lad who is walking towards him and recognizes the son of his tormentor.

*

I'm walking up the aisle and everyone's staring but I don't care. I see Annie with her mum halfway up on the left and, like an eejit, I forget we've fallen out. I wink at her. In return she gives me a cold stare and looks away. Good girl. Quick as I can I reach the family pew and I look across to the left and I see Bridget and I am frozen and I can't move at all and suddenly I hear a voice:

'Where the hell have you been?' But it's a blur, this voice, because all I can think about are Bridget's lovely breasts.

Then I can hear the old man again. 'Oi, Justin! I said, how did you get here?'

I suddenly come to my senses. 'Mother! On her way to Church. You left me behind,' says I, pushing past him to sit between Emma and Lucy.

'You were late, as per usual.' He's happy now. 'I never. She's going to Church again.'

'That's good,' says Emma who approves of going to Church even though it's a Proddie one.

I'm between the girls now and I whisper. 'She's really dressed. And that perfume – what a pong!'

'That's bad,' says Emma, strangely changing her mind. What's she on about?

'Scent, man, scent!' says Lucy. '*Perfume* is what the peasants call it.'

So I lift the tip of my nose to let her know I think she's a terrible snob and the old man nods at Father Luke, telling him to continue.

'My brothers and sisters, to prepare ourselves to celebrate the sacred mysteries,' he says, all slow, 'let us call to mind our sins.' Father Luke pauses and smiles, very pleased with himself. He doesn't know he's fighting a losing battle.

Suddenly all the congregation start at once at high speed, women and men, even the lads who stand at the back. It's like a sheep sale in Australia. 'I-confess-to-Almighty-God-and-to-you-my-brothers-and-sisters-that-I-have-sinned-through-my-own-fault-in-my-thoughts-and-in-my-words-in-what-I-have-done-and-in-what-I-have-failed-to-do.'

Poor old Father Luke has turned white as the locals continue.

'And-I-asked-blessed-Mary-ever-virgin-all-the-angels-and-saints-and-you-my-brothers-and-sisters-to-pray-for-me-to-the-Lord-our-God.' They're finished now and out of breath and happy as Larry, all of them. The old man smiles to himself and to the men behind who nod back, united in triumph. Poor old Father Luke looks totally gobsmacked.

Outside the church the old man shakes hands with the new priest. 'Forty-two minutes. Not bad ... for the first time.' A warning.

'Thank ... thank you, Mr Montague.' Another one bites the dust.

I'm watching the old man walk with the sisters towards the Jag, but out of the corner of one eye I'm also watching Annie as she gets onto the Dublin bus, which has just appeared. Annie's looking all serious and sad and she's doing a grand job as her parents look upset as well. Great. The bus pulls away. It's my turn now. I walk away from the Jag and across the road kicking the gravel and sulking and trying hard to look all forlorn and suicidal and I can hear the old man behind me commenting to everyone who'll listen, about me, of course. 'Pathetic!'

Then he shouts out to get my attention. '*Oi!* Justin?'

'Leave him alone,' says Emma. As if.

'If you're not back in half an hour, you'll miss lunch!' That would only be a punishment for you, you fat git. I reach the trees on the far side and I'm trying hard to go a little faster without him noticing and I wish he'd just get into his fecking Jew's canoe and go home. Hurry up please Dad, hurry or you'll ruin my brilliant plan. Just as I'm about to give up hope the Jag starts and he roars off down the road.

Now I'm running through the woods as hard as I can go and I'm smiling again because no one's looking. I grab a branch as a whip and now I'm winning the Grand National.

'*Coming to the post it's Carrickbeg chased by Ayala ridden by that great Irish jockey Pat Buckley ...*' I'm flying through the bushes being scratched alive by the branches and stung by the nettles and I'm beating myself with the stick as I run. '... *now Ayala's moving up. Can he make it? A hundred yards to go and Ayala's in front. He's going to win, he's going to win!*' I jump over a fence and '*He's won!*' onto the road, right into the path of the Dublin bus, which screeches to a halt in front of me.

The bus is moving again and I'm apologizing to the driver who, to give him his due, looks amused. Unfortunately, the conductor doesn't look very happy.

'Bold boy!' says the driver, trying to look serious.

'Thank you, sir, for stopping,' says I, all humble-like.

Mr Grumpy Conductor is not impressed. 'I'll sir you, you little skunt!'

The driver's still on my side though. 'Hold on now, Jimmy. He's just a kid running off some energies. Were you never one?'

I run upstairs quick out of harm's way. Annie stands at the top in fits of laughter. 'Just like Ronnie Delany winning Olympic gold,' she says.

'More like Milo O'Shea winning an Oscar. Poor Emma. She nearly cried for pitying me.' I pull out the wad of cash, very pleased with myself.

'Jesus, Mary and Joseph, you robbed the bank.'

'No. The old man. Hey, I've got a new one about poor old Paddy.'

'Sock it to me, Shakespeare.' Annie loves my little poems.

'*Paddy Kelly broke his belly, sliding on a lump of jelly ...*'

'Brilliant!' says Annie.

We're both repeating it, laughing: '*Paddy Kelly broke his belly, sliding on a lump of jelly. Paddy Kelly broke his belly, sliding on a lump of jelly.*'

Minutes later we're sitting right up the front of the bus. We're looking through the huge window and it's like going to the cinema and the bus seems to be going really fast when you're sitting up here like a fairground ride. I totally understand why Paddy Kelly likes them so much, these buses. Whenever there's a new design of double-decker Paddy, on his day off, will ride the bus to Dublin and back time and time again until it's dark. Once Paddy was reading his old newspapers late into the night, as he always does, when his eye catches an advertisement. '*CIÉ Mystery Bus Tour of the Countryside. £3. Lavish Picnic Included.*'

On this particular day Paddy Kelly sets off all excited to Dublin, to CIÉ headquarters. He pays his £3, nearly a week's wages, and away they go on the *Mystery Bus Tour of the Countryside,* Paddy and all these Dublin ladies. But where do they go on this mystery tour? All around the area where we live. Sadly for Paddy, he knew every inch of the ground the bus covered. At the end of the day, the bus heads back to Dublin and on its journey goes right past the lane on Golden Hill where Paddy lives with the old lady who looks after him. 'Let me off. Let me off,' mutters Paddy.

'No way,' answers the greasy Dublin driver in his greasy Dublin voice. 'I tuke twenty-tree people on this tewer and that's hew many I have to bring back. Rewels are rewels. So sit back dewen. *At wunce!*' Poor Paddy had to ride the bus the whole way to town and catch another one, all the way back home.

And so here we are, Annie and me, and we're up the front and singing and the only other people up here on the top of the 62a bus to Dublin are two old ladies who are loving it and tapping their seats as we sing away, the pair of us, in our best Dublin accents: '*I'll tell me ma, when I go home, the boys won't leave the girls alone. They pull my hair, they steal my comb, and that's alright till I go home. She is handsome, she is pretty, she's the belle of Belfast city. She's a courtin', one, two …*'

'Stop that racket!' Oh shite. Mr Grumpy Conductor is standing right over us, furious. 'Hold on, now. Hold on just a bleeding minute. I know you. You're a Montague, aren't you?'

'So?'

Then he sticks his ugly face right into mine and spits all over me, dirty bastard. 'So? So you're going to be a loud-mouthed gobshite just like your father.'

Well it's one thing me being rude about the old man but I'm not going to have some fecking Dublin gurrier insulting him.

'You're the fecking gobshite!'

The conductor grabs my ear and pulls it really hard and I practically wet myself as he splutters at me. 'I'm going to give you what for, you stuck up snotty little blow-in.'

'I'm not a blow-in. I was born here, I'm Irish! Do you hear? Irish!'

'If a cat has kittens in a fishmonger's it doesn't make them fish, does it?'

I'm lost for words but Annie isn't. 'Ah, but he *smells* of fish.' And now she's batting her beautiful eyes at the conductor. 'Mr Conductor? Justin's dad may be a little bit loud, just like that Murphy fella. You know Mr Murphy? Isn't he your boss?'

You liar, Annie. Brilliant! The conductor, suddenly nervy, lets go of my ear and now I'm rubbing it and trying at the same time to keep track of what Annie's up to.

'In fact, Justin, wasn't that Mr Murphy down at The Hall for a party just the other day? I'm sure Mr Murphy would love to hear how well you looked after us on the way to Dublin. Wouldn't he, Justin?'

'Oh he's always asking, so he is,' says I.

'Well?' asks the conductor, all subdued and quiet.

'Well what?'

'Where are youse two agitators getting off then? That's what.'

Annie hands him a half-crown, smiling away all innocent. 'Two tickets for Aston Quay. Thanks a million, sir.'

I much prefer going to Dublin on the bus. What I mean is, I hate going with the parents. Don't get me wrong, they're both really great drivers, but they go too fast and I always end up sitting on a copy of *The Irish Times* to try to stop being sick. It never works. Mum learnt her driving as a Wren in the war. As a result, because her father was an earl, she had two titles, not just one like all the other girls. She was *Leading Wren Lady Helen Browne*. Leading Wren was apparently the naval term for a corporal. Anyhow, when Mum is tanked up she's always telling us sob stories about how hard she had it in the war and how she lived in digs in Islington and how she had to drive every day all the way to Twickenham to pick up this admiral, her boss, and take him to the ministry. And how horrible he was to her. When I asked my Uncle Freddie, Mum's brother, who is now the Earl of Charlton, he gave me a totally different story to the one Mum had always bandied about.

'What utter nonsense! Your mother always did exaggerate. Your grandfather felt so sorry for Helen living in her frightful digs that he moved her out after just a week and gave her a double bedroom next to his suite at the Dorchester in Park Lane. On top of that, she persuaded the hotel manager to install the first ever air-conditioning unit. And the old admiral was so in love with Helen that he kept giving her days off and buying her wonderful lunches and theatre tickets.'

One thing about Mum is that when she drinks she never really gets out of control like the old man. She just starts slurring her words. Mum isn't the greatest mother in the world but I love her in a strange sort of a way and I wouldn't like anything to happen to her.

Not long ago one of the locals, a really nice fella called Johnny Rice, was killed in a car accident by a drunk driver. Johnny had taken the pledge as a youngster and had never had a drop of booze in his life. That made it all the worse, the fact that he was killed by someone who was absolutely plastered. Lucy, for some reason, knew the family better than any of us and was invited to the lying-in where the body was on display the night before the funeral. Mum overheard Lucy telling Emma that she was going and decided to come along as well.

So off they went, the three of them, Emma, Lucy and a more-than-tiddly Mum, to pay their respects to the family of poor Johnny. Apparently the coffin was open as Johnny didn't have any facial scars, and it was placed in the middle of the church. As they filed past the coffin, Mum stumbled and grabbed a hold of the side to stop herself falling. According to Lucy and Emma, the coffin almost rocked off its stand. Luckily the girls were on hand to steady it and stop it tumbling over. Emma said afterwards that it was bad enough being killed by a drunk but to be thrown out of your coffin by one afterwards would have been just too much for any poor soul to bear.

When Grandpa Charlton died, Granny kept on the suite at the Dorchester as her London flat. She was only there about once a month but I guess she didn't like to sleep in anybody else's bed. I never saw the rooms themselves but apparently Granny had all her own furniture and paintings up there so that she would feel at home when she went to town. When Granny's illness got really bad, Uncle Freddie designed a special hydraulic arm and a passenger lift. The lift itself was at Charlton, hidden behind a tapestry, and it went right up into her bedroom. The special hydraulic arm, appearing out of the door of her Rolls-Royce, would grab the wheelchair and hoik it into the car. From that time on, Granny could get into her wheelchair in her bedroom and never have to get out of it again until she was in her suite at the Dorchester.

Uncle Freddie also had rooms at the Dorchester when he was young. (Lucy told me this as she always knew all the gossip. And if she didn't, she'd just make some up.) Anyway, she made me swear not to tell anyone as it was a family scandal. Freddie, in his younger days, had inherited the family problem and used to knock back the gin. When he was on a bender he would hole up in his room at the hotel and drink himself stupid.

The Dorchester put up with his ways because the family were such good clients but one time Freddie was so drunk, he came out into the corridor waving his cane and attacked some big American film star, shouting, 'Get out of my house, *damn you!*' Well, that was the end of that. The Dorchester asked him, politely, to vacate his rooms and he gave in like a lamb because he didn't want a scandal.

Ten

If you can't get rid of the family skeleton,
you may as well make it dance.
George Bernard Shaw

Sunday, 30 June 1963

Summer dust flying, the black Jaguar growls sweetly as it careers down the avenue at high speed. Bobby may be driving fast, but he's in good humour. He's 'sorted' the new priest without any real trouble, and Helen is going to Church again. The Mark II slides to a halt, gravel flying, and the girls pile out.

Bridget stands waiting. Bobby jumps out. 'Hello there, Bridget. Lunch ready? I'm starved.'

'Yes sir. It is. And Lady Helen asked me to tell you not to wait for her.'

Bobby feels deflated. 'Oh right. There's no rush.'

'Since when?' Emma is suspicious. 'Where is she, exactly, Bridget?'

'Mrs Mullins asked if she, Her Ladyship I mean, would go straight to Kildare Hospital after Mass, as she couldn't have visitors after two. Her Ladyship said she would go after Church and probably wouldn't be back until tea.' Lucy and Emma exchange knowing looks. Long gone are the days

when Helen bothered to go and visit the sick in hospital.

'Probably?'

'That's what she said, Her Ladyship. Probably.'

'We'll wait half an hour. She'll be here. She loves Sunday roast.'

At that precise moment, Lady Helen's black Triumph Spit-fire, top down, whizzes along a country lane. The Triumph shoots past a sign. 'Dublin City Centre. 15 Miles'. Beside it, pointing in the opposite direction, is another sign. 'Kildare Town. 23 Miles'. Helen's brown hair flies wildly in the breeze. She has a smile on her face but she's not relaxed. She is excited, terribly excited, at the thought of what's going to happen to her when she reaches St Stephen's Green.

Emma, Lucy and Bobby are sitting on the front lawn on the old brown wicker chairs, reading the Sunday papers. Bobby is distracted. He is trying to focus on a half-naked photo of Christine Keeler, the prostitute at the centre of the Profumo scandal, which had just about brought down the Conservative government across the water in England. But his mind is elsewhere as he keeps checking his watch and listening for Helen's car.

'What about Annie?' asks Emma.

'I've made up my mind.'

'She's not a thief!'

'Oh, come on,' says Bobby. 'Pull the other one. You really think I believed that cock-and-bull about her coming to meet you?'

'Justin's crazy about her,' says Lucy, trying not to raise her voice.

'No, *he's not. He loves her,*' says Emma, in her usual blunt manner.

'Balderdash! Love? What the hell does a thirteen-year-old know about love!' Bobby is getting more wound up.

Emma, with a determined look on her face, takes out the package and opens it.

'Oh shite,' says Lucy.

Emma hands the gold cigarette case to Bobby.

'Where the hell did you find that? Your mother will be thrilled.'

'Annie found it.'

'Little fecker!'

'Ask me where she got it,' continues Emma.

'What does that matter? She stole it, didn't she?'

I wish she had, says Lucy to herself.

Emma drops the bombshell. 'An English gentleman in a sports car ...'

'Bridget!' yells Bobby, interrupting something he definitely does not want to hear. Bridget appears almost immediately. 'Where's our lunch?'

'Whenever you're ready, sir.'

'I am ready. Otherwise I wouldn't be asking, would I?'

Bridget goes to fetch the lunch, wondering if she will ever get off for the afternoon and her trip to Dublin.

'Come on then Cromwell, you old fool,' says Bobby as he marches towards the house. He is determined to keep up a good front. The Rottweiler follows and the girls join him, walking either side. 'It's taken Cook bloody years to get the Yorkshire pudding right.'

'Dad, are you okay?' asks Lucy.

'Never better.'

'Don't you get it?' Emma forces the issue.

Lucy tries to stop her. 'Cool it, man.'

'She's at it again.'

Bobby stops. 'That's enough!'

Emma digs the knife in and twists. 'What about Justin? Isn't it about time he knew? Everyone else does.'

Bobby, looking really hurt and with his head down, lumbers through the door.

Eleven

When I die, Dublin will be written in my heart.

Sean O'Casey

Sunday, 30 June 1963

We're in Dublin, Annie and myself, and we're near St Stephen's Green right in the centre of the city. Annie grabs me and looks up and yelps: 'Oh, would ya look? Maureen Potter!' It's The Gaiety Theatre and the sign says, 'Ulysses *by James Joyce. Starring Maureen Potter and Milo O'Shea.*'

God, I love Maureen Potter. She's the best actress in the whole of Ireland and the kids just worship her. We go every Christmas to see her in the panto. In one thing I saw, Maureen played this Dublin lady who has a son called Christy. (Mind you, every taxi driver in Dublin is called Christy.) In the story she takes her twelve-year-old Christy to the Phoenix Park, to see a balloon race. But Christy's a real eejit and gets into a basket while his mother's not looking and the rope breaks and there's the balloon disappearing into the sky with Maureen, standing in the middle of the stage, calling up at him in her strongest Dublin accent: 'Christy? Christy? Will ya come down outta that baloowen, will ya?'

'I've seen her loads of times,' says I, showing off.

'You are *so* lucky,' says Annie to me, all envious.

'I saw her last week too, on the tellies, Maureen with Jimmy O'Dea. God, it was brilliant. She had us in stitches.'

'Lucky you,' says Annie, still looking up at the theatre sign. 'Ulysses? Wasn't he a strong man? Like in a circus?'

'As if I'd know.' I wish she wouldn't ask me questions like that. Just because I have a posh voice and go to school in England it doesn't mean I know everything.

'I've never been to a play or a panto,' says Annie, all sorry for herself.

'More importantly, Miss Cassidy, you've never been to tea at the Shelbourne. So move it, baby!' That cheered her up.

We're hurrying now and just coming onto the Green past the market stalls and I love the noise and the market ladies shouting. As we reach the stalls there's one lady I know really well, Aggie, and she's wider than she's tall. If I had to guess I would say she eats more than just the fruit she sells. She's practically bursting out of her white apron. Aggie's doing her usual pitch to the crowd. '*Pears, apples or chocolate! Oranges, luvvely oranges!*' Suddenly Aggie's seen me and now she's yelling, 'Ah, Justin. Hew are ya, luv?'

Annie is really surprised. 'She knows you?'

I take some change out of my pocket and whisper aside: 'That's Aggie. She doesn't listen, Aggie. Watch!' I lead Annie up to the stall and I start perusing the fruit display all serious as though I'm terribly interested. Aggie wants to chat, of course.

'Ah luv. How are ye ma and ye da?'

'Fine thanks, Aggie,' says I. And then a little quieter. 'Both dead.' I wink at Annie.

'Ah that's grand,' says Aggie, totally missing the point. 'Now, what'll ya have?' Annie's trying really hard not to laugh.

'Just the two pears please,' says I, all straight-faced.

'Of course, luv. And an extra one only for you, pet.' Aggie squeezes my cheek as usual, which I hate, but put up with as she'll be offended if I say anything.

I give her a shilling. 'Keep the change, please. Thanks Aggie, bye.'

'Bye luv. God bless.'

'Told you,' says I to Annie, all smug, as we walk off.

'Both dead? You're a loony.' Annie and I are laughing away as we continue onto the Green towards the Shelbourne and we can hear Aggie still roaring away behind us: '*Pears, apples or chocolate! Oranges, luvvely oranges!*'

'A shilling? You gave her a whole shilling? Are you mad or what?' Annie is amazed.

'The old man pays much more, at least double.'

'Why?'

'Guilt,' says I.

'Guilt?'

'That's what Lucy says.'

'About what?'

'Being rich, I suppose.'

'Oh.'

We're walking along the Green towards the Shelbourne and I'm salivating at the thought of their lovely cakes and cream when Annie suddenly stops and points across the road.

'Isn't that your mother's car?'

I stop myself and look across and there it is – a black Triumph Spitfire just like Mum's. I can't see the number plate as it's sideways, but there's no point.

'It couldn't be.'

'How come?'

'She went to Kildare, to visit a friend in the hospital.'

'Oh,' says Annie and off we run into the Shelbourne Hotel and I'm glad I've loads of dosh because it's really, really expensive, tea at the Shelbourne. I'm still wondering about the black Triumph. I've never seen another one before in Ireland. I must remember to tell Mum.

*

On the first floor of the Shelbourne Hotel, Lady Helen Montague, Hermes scarf almost covering her face, looks around. The coast is clear. Helen knocks on the tall mahogany doors of the George Moore Suite. Her heart beats fast. She's so excited she could scream.

*

I lead Annie into the beautiful lobby and I know she'll be impressed but I remain all cool.

'Janey!' says Annie, flabbergasted and staring around her.

'Come on. This way. Oh yeah, see over there? That door? In there, that's where Michael Collins drafted the Irish Constitution in 1922.' But then something surprises me, as I peep in.

'God almighty,' says I softly to myself. I stop in my tracks like I've been shot, and I'm staring and I can't help it. There's a man and a woman grabbing one another like they haven't seen each other in years. And it makes me feel all strange, watching this. All funny peculiar.

*

In the George Moore Suite, the Rake stares at Helen. He has a hard look on his face, and he stands, arms folded, between the two French windows that lead to the balcony overlooking the Green.

Helen is breathless. 'Roger? What?'

She knows exactly what, because it's what she always wants.

Roger, leaping forward, grabs Helen by her beautiful hair, throws her on the bed, and pushes her face down into a pillow. 'You dirty bitch! I know you're wet! I know you are, you tart!'

Helen moans, as Roger pulls up her skirt and rips down her silk underwear. His other hand pins her to the bed. Helen gasps. 'I'm going to fuck you till you scream, you slut!'

*

Annie follows me into the Lord Mayor's Lounge and I wait at the entrance for the head waiter to greet us. 'Just like home,' says Annie, staring up at the enormous crystal chandelier hanging from the centre of the ceiling.

The head waiter appears with his hair all Brylcreemed down and shiny and black, and he's slick as well, just like the hair. 'Good afternoon, sir. Two for tea?'

'Thank you.'

'Excuse me, Mister,' says Annie, all polite.

'Yes, miss?'

'What do ya call a Kerryman who hangs upside down off the ceiling?'

'Young lady?'

'What do ya call a Kerryman who hangs upside down off the ceiling? *Sean D'Olear!*' Annie points up at the enormous lights.

'Get it?'

He gets it, but I think he's heard it before as he's not laughing.

'Yes, two please,' says I, politely and firmly.

The head waiter bows and theatrically waves an arm.

'Thank you, sir. This way. And madam?' Now he's taking the mickey out of Annie. 'Such an honour to have that great actress Miss Maureen Potter in our humble lounge.' Good for him.

'Have you ever seen her, Maureen Potter?'

'Seen her? Young lady, if I had a shilling for every time Miss Potter ordered scones, strawberry jam and clotted cream, I'd be a very moneyed man. She's in most days before her performance. Now, will here do?' He indicates a yellow silky sofa facing a brown and very polished coffee table.

'Thanks a million,' says Annie. 'My mum's called Maureen.'

'How very interesting. Between you and me. Once ...' he leans forward and whispers like in a conspiracy, '... Miss Potter came for tea with *Tyrone Power!* And they sat at this very table, on this very sofa. There you are now,' he says, very pleased with himself.

'Tyrone Power? He is totally gorgeous.'

'No, he isn't! He's old!' says I.

'Gotcha!' teases Annie.

Feck. Why do I get so jealous?

We're sitting on the sofa facing the main door, feeling important, and the head waiter has turned out to be a real laugh. 'I'll let you know the moment Miss Potter arrives. I'll have a word and see if I can introduce you. Now, your wish is my command. What would you like for tea?'

'What's good enough for Miss Potter, is good enough for us,' says I.

'Oh yes please, sir,' says Annie, breathlessly.

'Scones, jam and clotted cream, it is then. Might I also recommend hot drinking chocolate?'

'Oh yes, please,' says Annie again. 'Thanks a million.'
Now he's off to get our order and I'm watching him go with
admiration. 'God, isn't he great?'

*

'Wonderful.' Lady Helen lies back on the bed, dishevelled,
eyes blazing.

Roger, lying exhausted beside her, is pleased with his
performance but wishes Helen would occasionally like something a little more romantic. He sips from a Bloody Mary.

'Was it really?'

'What do you think?' She smiles, and Roger grabs his
chance, the only chance to once again broach the subject
that means so much to him.

'Helen, darling? Have you thought about what I said?
Lamu Island. Imagine! Sunshine every day, lovely African
people, the Indian Ocean at weekends. Honestly, darling,
you wouldn't believe it. It's like going back a thousand years.
Stunning blue sea, old dhows, friendly Arabs, dolphins, tur-
tles, and ...'

'And what?' says Helen, wishing that Roger would just
shut up and enjoy the moment.

'We'd have loads of servants.'

'I have loads of servants.'

'The boy can come with us.'

Helen takes a Cocktail Sobranie from the pack and
lights it. Then she remembers when she last had her cigarette case.

'Oh my God. Have you got it?'

'Got what?'

'My cigarette case, of course. Didn't I leave it in your
MG? I'm sure I did.'

'Oh shit!' Roger looks worried. 'You did.'

'So? Where is it?'

Moments later, Helen is striding furiously down the main staircase into the lobby. She's so annoyed she's even forgotten that they shouldn't be seen together.

'Are you always so stupid?' Roger, following close behind, hardly has a chance to answer.

'A pretty girl, right at your gates. The front ones.'

'You ass!'

'I'm so sorry.'

'No, you're bloody not. You did it on purpose!' she hisses.

'Christ, darling, I just wanted to get a look. There's nothing wrong with that. After all, he is mine, isn't he?'

'I told you, stay away from him!' Roger thinks it better just to remain silent. Whatever he says will only be wrong. 'Well? Describe her.'

'A stunner. Too young, of course.'

'I didn't ask whether you'd like to sleep with her, although I wouldn't be surprised. Brunette, red hair, blonde?'

Roger's face is in shock. 'Like her,' he says.

'Like whom?'

'That's her!' Roger points into the Lord Mayor's Lounge. 'Now, we'll find out. Oh yes, we will,' he says as he strides in.

But before he can get through the door, Helen grabs him and pushes him round the corner against the wall, out of sight.

'Hey!' says Roger, protesting.

'Don't you dare!'

'Why ever not?'

'She's with the boy.'

*

Annie and I are sitting there having a great old time eating
cakes and strawberries and scones and clotted cream and
Annie's gawping at her chandelier and I'm looking across the
room and I see that couple again, the ones from the lobby,
and I suddenly realize what it is that confused me about
what they were up to.

'Listen,' says I to Annie, all serious. 'Do you think we're
different? You and me?'

'Have you looked in your pants lately?'

'Ha, ha. Very funny. What I mean is. Once I remember
when you went to visit your uncle in Donegal and you came
back ...'

'Yeh?'

'I saw your parents. They, they threw their arms around
you. Your mother actually cried.'

'So?'

'What's it like?'

'I dunno. Just normal I suppose.' Well, it doesn't look
normal to me. It looks fecking weird.

'Annie? Did you ever watch those American films where
they live in white houses with porches and they all have big
lawns that go straight down to the road with brand new red
bicycles flying everywhere, and everyone knows everyone
and there's never a cloudy day? Big fridges in all the kitchens
and hanging out at the ice-cream parlour?'

'Lovely.'

'That's where I'd like to live. Wouldn't you? Annie?'
Annie's not listening and the cup of hot drinking chocolate
in her hand starts shaking and I know she's going to drop it,
the clumsy cow, all over the silky yellow sofa. I grab it quick,
the cup, and just in bloody time, thank heavens.

'Oh, my God! Hello Mister.'

Annie's staring up like she's seen a ghost and I look up and there's this big man standing over me and Annie and I've never seen him before but something makes me feel I have.

'Aren't you going to introduce me, young lady?'

'This is Justin. Justin *Montague*,' says Annie, all nervous and emphasizing my surname for some strange reason.

'Hello, Justin. I'm Roger.' So I jump up and take his hand.

'Hello sir. How do you do?' But he keeps a hold of my hand and doesn't let go of squeezing it and it's all sweaty, his palm is, but I don't want to be rude and pull away.

'Emma has it,' says Annie quickly to my surprise.

'Oh dear,' says this Roger fella, looking worried.

'Emma? Emma has what?' Annie doesn't answer me. What the fuck is she on about?

'May I sit?' asks Mr Clammy Hands.

'Please do sir,' says I, moving the bag of pears from the sofa.

'Thank you … Justin,' he says, staring at me. I mean *really* staring. 'I say. When's your birthday?'

'My birthday? June 26th. I was just thirteen, sir.'

'You're a good-looking young boy.' I'm looking at Annie and we're thinking the same thing about this weirdo and we're trying not to laugh. So before we do, we make our excuses and leave.

*

Roger is alone. On his lap sits the bag of pears. He munches one, distracted, and even though he realizes he is dribbling pear juice down one side of his chin, he doesn't care. Roger's life has changed in one moment. He has just met his son, his only child, for the first time ever. He doesn't know what to

feel and he hardly hears the words of the head waiter who is
now standing over him.

'Afternoon tea, sir?'

'What? No, thank you. Armagnac please, Laballe, Cha-
teau Laballe. A double. No. Make it a double, double.'

'Certainly, sir.' The head waiter turns to leave.

'One moment. That boy? Do you think we look alike,
him and I? The one that was just here with the young gal?'

'Oh yes sir, of course. I'll get your brandy, sir. You'll
feel much better.' The head waiter walks off, muttering to
himself. It must be the moon. Jesus, the boy is the spitting
image of his da.

*

I'm in shock because I'm clutching a ten-pound note, a
whole ten pounds, as we walk back down St Stephen's Green
towards Grafton Street.

'Dirty skunt!' says I, all disgusted with the perv.

'Who gives a shite? Ten whole pounds! God, give us
twenty, we'll arrange an orgy!' Roaring with laughter we're
running off down the street towards the Green Cinema.

When you want to go on a date in Ireland, you ask a
girl to the pictures. Once you've met them, probably at a
hop. I went to my first hop in the local town hall about six
months ago. Everyone was away and Bridget was desperate
to go and didn't want to go alone. I was happy to oblige and
in the end was really pleased I did. It was a great laugh. All
the lads were sitting on these long wooden benches down
one side of the hall, facing the women sitting on the other.
One of these lads, Declan Flanagan, a spotty bank clerk, had
noticed Bridget and was desperate to ask her to dance. All
his friends kept nudging him to get across and speak to her

and finally he got up the courage. Declan took off his cap and across he comes to Bridget and mutters, 'Would you like a dance?'

Off they went, flying around the floor while the local show band played an Elvis song called 'Kiss Me Quick'. When the music finished, the happy lad brings Bridget back to her place where I was sitting with all the ladies. As they arrive back, Declan says to your one, to Bridget.

'Would you like a mineral? Or would you like to go the toilet?'

Anyway, Bridget looks Declan up and down for what seems like a very long time and then replies.

'I think I'll just go the toilet, thanks anyway.'

The poor Flanagan lad looked devastated and I couldn't figure out why. Christ, she only wanted to go the bathroom. It couldn't be that bad, could it? I soon found out the truth on the way home when Bridget explained. Apparently it was a signal, this wanting to go to the toilet. If Bridget had wanted to spend more time with Declan, she would have just accepted the offer of the mineral. She didn't fancy him, not at all. So she went to the toilet even though she explained that she hadn't really wanted to go at all.

Twelve

*Anybody can be good in the country. There
are no temptations there.*

Oscar Wilde

Sunday, 30 June 1963

We're inside the Green Cinema, Annie and me, and it's only
half full, which is surprising because I just read in *The Guinness Book of Records* for 1962 that the Irish go to the cinema more than anyone else in the world: twenty-six times
per person, per year.

Annie and I are sitting, feet up, watching advertisements
and shovelling popcorn and we can't help joining in on the
jingle for the bread that gets delivered to us in a van. *'Johnston, Mooney, and O'Brien, Make the best bread, bread you
can rely on. It's Johnston, Mooney, and O'Brien, the favourite family pan! Da da!'* And we're laughing away at how
funny we are and people are staring but we don't care. If
you've had to tangle with my old man on a daily basis nothing scares you. Or everything does, if I'm honest.

A little later and the main programme is on. Annie's eyes
are out on stalks, and I jump up out of my seat like a real
hero to protect her, and now I'm pointing my pistols like
John bloody Wayne.

'Get back!' I yell at Annie, as I stand in front of her and I start to shoot the scary birds on the big screen. '*Pow, pow! Pow, pow!*' And some people are looking round in their seats, disgusted, but I don't care as I've got ten pounds in my pocket. '*Pow, pow!*'

And now the whole cinema is staring. '*Pow, pow!*'

Annie grabs me and pulls me back down into my seat. 'Nutter!'

I'm sure she's thrilled and proud of me for being such a hero. We're watching again and it is frightening, as poor old Tippi Hedren gets all blooded being scratched and pecked by birds that have gone mad. Annie grabs my arm for safety and I love it as no one can see. I just wish I had the nerve to kiss her as well.

Anyway, I'm just happy to have enough cash to take Annie to the cinema, not something I can always do. I used to have a friend, Walter Cosgrove, and Walter's parents were really rich and owned most of the cinemas in Dublin. The only money I ever had was from working on the farm, and as I only got half-wages for working my arse off I never ended up with much in my pocket and I couldn't afford to take Annie to the cinema, something she really loved. Luckily Walter fancied Annie. So Walter and I came to a gentlemen's agreement. He would get us the tickets and we would sit either side of Annie. It was quite funny as Annie and I would have our eyes glued to the screen and Walter would have his glued to Annie. Walter once said to me:

'Gosh, Justin. She's lovely, Annie. I just wish I had the nerve to take someone like that home.'

I didn't know whether to laugh or cry. What he was basically saying was that he liked Annie enough to bring her to his house but wouldn't have the nerve to introduce her to his parents as she wasn't from the same kind of background.

In the end, Annie got sick at being gawped at by Walter so I had to revert to stealing money from the old man's holiday cupboard to pay for our visits to the pictures.

This holiday cupboard, as I called it, was in his dressing room above his sock drawers. As soon as the parentals came back from one of their many holliers, the old man would just grab all his foreign currency and throw it up on the top shelf. He was too bloody lazy to bother changing it. About once every two years he would grab the whole lot and take it into Dublin and have it converted. There was always piles of it lying around, mainly French francs or Canadian or American dollars. I would sneak in, grab a bundle and take it to the bank in Dublin. It was very exciting because I never knew how much I would get and I always justified it in my mind that it was Mum's family money and therefore more mine than his. I guess it is still stealing so I'll tell the priest eventually. That should make his day.

The old man himself always had problems with the bank. Well, that's not altogether true. In fact it was normally the other way round. They had problems with him. They were terrified. One time the new head bank manager in St Stephen's Green wrote to him. He just wanted to go over everything and discuss the huge overdraft. Apparently the old man had received a very polite letter from this particular new manager, suggesting that he, the manager, could come out to visit the old man at The Hall or if that didn't suit, he would be delighted to 'meet you in town and give you luncheon at the Kildare Street Club'. A very charming letter by all accounts.

But the old man didn't see it that way. He saw it as a threat and went berserk and wrote back a stinging reply saying that he would go and meet the new manager 'when he was good and ready and not before!' And if the bank manager was 'stupid enough to mention his overdraft again, he would move banks'. I guess the old man knew he held the power as Grandpa Charlton was a director of the very same bank in England.

Lucy saw the actual reply that he sent and it ended like this: 'To put it in simple terms you might be capable of under-standing – *don't cut the udders off a good milking cow!*'

As we walk out of the Green Cinema I check the time but Annie's still thinking about the film. 'Watch out! Keep your eyes open!' she yelps, all fake-scared and looking up to the sky as though we're about to be horribly savaged by a few scrawny old Dublin seagulls.

I glance at my watch and realize to my horror that we're late. 'Oh shite, Annie. The last bus. *Run!*'

Now we're running hard holding hands down Grafton Street towards Aston Quay to catch the 62a. I hear someone hooting their car behind us and I look back to see if they're hooting at us but Annie says all funny, 'Don't! Probably more perverts.'

I'm still running but looking back and I can't believe my eyes and I stop suddenly and I'm still holding Annie's hand and I'm much stronger than her because of riding racehorses and Annie practically flies in through the door of Bewley's coffee house because I stopped so quick. 'Jesus, Annie, sorry. It's Donal. Look!'

The Jaguar pulls up, all slow of course, with Donal driving and Bridget in the passenger seat. Bridget thinks it's hilarious seeing the pair of us. 'Would youse two like a lift or are you eloping?'

'Eloping,' says Annie. She loves Bridget.

'I wouldn't be surprised. Hop in!'

A little later the Jag crawls down a country lane. Annie and I are in the back, and Annie leans forward over the red leather seat, which is just like a sofa, and points at Bridget's large bag. 'Shopping?'

'Of course,' says Bridget.

'What did you buy?'

'Glue, what else? To fix a certain Chinese vase.' Bridget's got this funny-serious look on her gob, that look she has when she's taking the mickey. Annie gets the joke straight away.

'Sorry Bridget. I couldn't help it. Mr Montague gave me such a fright ...'

'I wouldn't worry yerself. It was only a fake.'

Annie makes the sign of the cross and looks heaven-wards. 'Thank you, God.'

Donal decides it's time to make an announcement.

'Justin? I was informed by the boss man that you two weren't to be seeing each other.'

'Donal will say nothing, I can assure you,' says Bridget, staring daggers at Donal.

'What about youse two, Donal?' asks Annie. Christ, she's got a nerve that one.

'*Mr* Sheridan to you, Annie Cassidy,' says Donal, furi-ous at Annie's impertinence.

'Sorry, *Mr* Sheridan,' says Annie, not sorry at all.

Donal doesn't like Annie's cheek. Not one iota. 'You're a bold girl, Annie Cassidy, and very pass-remarkable. I was giving Bridget a lift to visit her sister. She's married in Blackrock.'

'Everyone's married in Blackrock. Anyway, Donal's engaged himself,' says Bridget.

Annie and I are stunned.

'No!' says Annie.

'Since when?' asks I.

'May,' says Donal.

'1959,' says Bridget.

'Bloody hell! Four whole years?' says Annie.

Now Bridget's having fun and teasing Donal. 'Poor woman. When are you going to do it?'

'Maybe next year. As you know ...' and now Donal's looking in the mirror at us two, '... I don't like to rush things.'

We nearly wet ourselves laughing. I have never, ever, heard Donal make a joke, especially about himself. It was brilliant.

Donal had a cousin, Declan Reynolds, a really lovely man. He wasn't serious like Donal and was always very kind. Declan was an electrician in Clondakin and used to come and sort out all our wiring and service the generator. I mean, when you lived in this part of the world, the power was always going off and that would mean a disaster in the milking parlour. Imagine milking a hundred and fifty cows by hand: your fingers would drop off! So because of the farm and the racehorses we had our own diesel-powered generator.

As soon as the power went out, the old man would lumber out with his torch to go and wind up the wheel and get the generator started. You could hear him cursing away about bloody Ireland and the bloody Irish. But he wasn't really being honest. I'm sure that it made him really happy, made him feel like a real man, to have to go out in the middle of a stormy night to save us and the animals from a terrible fate.

I think Declan realized what a hard time I had, so he used to take me pike fishing. I was always a bit suspicious of people like Declan. After all my own father doesn't even like me so why would someone like Declan take an interest? Was he a perv or just trying to get in the old man's good books? I just couldn't help thinking it because I don't really trust many people, but I do feel bad for having had those thoughts, especially about such a kind man.

One day in the middle of winter, Declan took me down to a fishing spot at a place called Polauphouca, which is Irish for 'the devil's hole'. So there we were fishing away with these poor minnows hooked up alive to tempt the pike, when suddenly this enormous monster grabs the line. It took me about half an hour to get the bloody fish in. My fingers were frozen and I was exhausted. Mind you, so was the poor pike. We put the dead pike with all its huge crocodile teeth into the bucket between my knees on the passenger's side of Declan's old car and we drove home, thrilled: at least I was thrilled until the pike suddenly came alive and leapt out of the bucket onto my knees. I nearly died of fright. We ate the pike the next day as kedgeree with eggs and rice and all that. It was delicious.

Sometimes in the summer, especially on a Thursday, I would go and shoot a rabbit and run straight away as quick as I could down to the river. Then I would take the rabbit and hang it with a piece of string, which I had stolen from the old potting-shed. I would hang the rabbit upside down by its back legs right over the clear river water with the blood all dripping down. In no time at all the flies would be swarming round and then all the trout and perch would come to get to the flies. Very soon I would have a bank full of lovely fresh fish, which I would take home and stick in the fridge to save for eating the next day, a Friday. I loved cutting off the heads and tails and removing the slimy guts with my middle fingers.

We always had fish on Fridays. We weren't allowed anything else. If we bought the fish from a shop, it was generally days old and smelt rotten. Donal's driving didn't really help – it could be fresh when he collected it in Dublin and rotten by the time he eventually got back to The Hall. If I remembered to go fishing on a Thursday and come back with a big enough basket to feed the family on the Friday, I was the most popular person in the house. Nobody shouted at me on those days. No way, Jose.

The river that runs through our land is called the Liffey and it flows out of the mountains right past us and on to Dublin and then into the Irish Sea. It looks filthy in Dublin, although, to be fair, that could just be the strong tides stirring all the sand and mud from the bottom. But where it comes through our land, the Liffey is really great. And I don't just fish there: I swim.

When we get a hot summer like last year, the river is brilliant. I would go down with Lucy at least twice a day. We'd run down the avenue through a small narrow iron gate and get into the Daisy Meadows, which meant brushing past all these nettles, then down to the beach. Honestly, we have a beach with real sand, right where the water is shallow and rushes past. From there we could either float down left into the deep pool full of trout and perch, or walk up to the right where there was a lovely area just like a large swimming pool called Magee's Pool. Apparently it was named after a man called Magee who drowned when fishing there. If you followed the river from there and went uphill, you would come to the source of the river near Mount Kippure, whereas if you followed the river in the other direction, you would travel about sixty-five miles and end up in Dublin.

From the age of seven I used to catch the bus by myself all the way to Dublin and get off, walk to O'Connell Street, and go to have egg and chips. There's nothing like egg and chips. If they were going to execute me tomorrow like poor Kevin Barry, I would order egg and chips as my final meal. After the egg and chips, which were sometimes covered in sugar, I would probably go to the Grafton Cinema and then finally finish the day in an amusement arcade. I loved this particular machine where you had a steering wheel and you drove a car faster and faster on this television until it crashed. I wasn't ever very good at it but it was great fun and made a fantastic noise when you had a pile-up.

One time when I was just nine I got chatting away in the arcade to an interesting man who told me that he also enjoyed the cars. While we were chatting he told me how he was in charge of the camera at all the sporting events for Telefís Éireann. Then he turned the chat to what I was up to.

'It's really hard, isn't it?'

'No, not really, I'm just not very good at it,' says I, all modest.

'No, not that. *This!*' he says, as it suddenly dawns on me that he's touching my dick from outside my shorts and I hadn't even noticed. Dirty bastard! So I made my excuses and left, very bloody sharp, and took the bus home.

I was dying to tell everyone about this weirdo but I didn't dare. If I had done I could just imagine the old man making a big song and dance, probably at a dinner party where I would be hanging around being made to serve drinks to show what a great job he had done bringing up his children. There would be a lull in the conversation and he'd say something like: 'Did you hear about Justin the other day? He was picking up old queers in O'Connell Street. Jesus, he'll have to grow up quick and stop looking like a big girl!'

Thirteen

This suspense is terrible. I hope it will last.
Oscar Wilde

Sunday, 30 June 1963

It is evening at The Hall, but still light. A flight of pigeons swoops across the shadowed roof, heading for the safety of the forest to rest up for the night. Justin walks fast towards the front door.

Just around the corner, the Jaguar pulls up in the yard. Bridget and Annie get out. Bridget takes her shopping and walks towards the house, calling over her shoulder: 'Bye Annie, thanks Donal. Thanks a million now.'

'My pleasure, Bridget,' *says Donal, in his usual Kerry drawl.*

'Thanks, Mr Sheridan,' *says Annie, not pushing it too far.*

'A word, please?' *Annie stops.* 'Stay away from Justin,' *says Donal, firmly.*

'What? Why?'

'Because the boss man said so, and because you should know your place.'

'Which, which place?' *Annie is shocked.*

'You are one of us, Annie. Not one of them.'

Annie feels like she's been stabbed in the heart. 'Yes sir. I'll remember. And hopefully one day, when Mr Montague dies and Master Justin takes over, I'm sure he'll give me a job, as a parlour maid.' She storms off. Donal shakes his head. She will get her comeuppance, he thinks to himself. She needs to learn a lesson before it's too late.

In the dining room at The Hall, Emma, Lucy, Helen, Bobby and Cromwell are eating. There's a pregnant silence. Bobby wants everything to be normal. He hopes that, if he says nothing, the problem will just disappear. And it would, if he didn't have that damn cigarette case. Lucy, worried about her father, cracks a joke to cheer him up. 'Knock knock?'

No answer.

'Dad? Come on, man! Knock, knock?'

'Go on. Who's there?'

'Siobhan.'

'Siobhan who?'

'Shove on your knickers, your mother's coming.' Bobby laughs weakly as the door opens.

*

I'm late and I'll be in trouble but then I always am, so who gives a shit? I open the door and everyone stares at me and I blurt out, 'Sorry, sorry.'

Feck it! I'm beginning to sound like a bloody Englishman.

'Hello, old cock. Where have you been?' asks the old man. Are you fucking kidding? Why's he being so nice? Is he drunk?

'Town,' says I, all cautious.

'Dublin?'

'Yup. To see a film.'

Now it's Mum's turn to shock me. 'Did you have a good time, darling?'

'Yeah, yes, thanks.'

'Ah, let me guess. *Hud?*' asks the old man, all excited.

'No Dad. *The Birds.* Hitchcock. Real scary.'

'Don't you like Westerns?' asks the old man, looking disappointed. I shake my head.

'Extraordinary.'

It's all quiet now and nobody's saying anything and Mary the new maid is clearing and the old man is watching her, all leery like. 'Where's Bridget?'

'It's her afternoon off, sir.'

'She had one last week.'

'No, sir. Excuse me, sir. That was the week before, it was, sir.'

'All right. Don't stand there, gawping. Pour Her Ladyship's wine.'

'Sir.'

Then Mum says something quite extraordinary. 'No. I'm fine, just fine.'

'Time for the news then.' The old man gets up and lumbers to the door, followed by Cromwell. Even Cromwell looks subdued. He seems to have forgotten all about this morning, thank God, when I slobbered at him through the window of the Jag.

'I'll join you in a minute, darling, I promise,' says Her Majesty. What the fuck is going on? Everyone's behaving so oddly.

The door shuts and I'm lost. 'What's up? Why's he being so nice?'

'He's always nice to you, darling,' says Mum, sweet as anything.

'Since when?'

'I know he shouts sometimes but it means nothing. He adores you.'

'I'll remember that, *Mother,* next time he calls me a useless little fucker.' Now I feel better. I've added some real conversation to the table and I'm on a flow and I turn to the sisters with the gossip. 'Hey uglies? I met a pervert.'

'Where?' asks Emma, all a tremor for some reason. Before I can answer, Mum tries to change the subject, just when it's becoming interesting.

'Do you think I should give Bridget more days off?'

'Mother?' says Emma, with that hard look she gets sometimes.

'Yes darling?'

'Do you even know where the kitchen is?'

'That's very unkind.'

'And Justin,' says Lucy, quick as a flash.

'Yes darling?' says I, just as witty.

'Do you even know what a pervert is?'

'He was shaking and had wet clammy hands and wouldn't let go.'

'Yuck,' says Lucy.

'That's a pervert, isn't it?'

Mum gets up to leave. 'I'd better keep your father company.'

'That'll make a change,' spits Emma, sticking the knife in. We often give Mum a hard time when the old man's not around.

Mum, ignoring Emma, walks to the door slowly. 'Where was he?' asks Lucy, very insistent.

'Whom?'

'The perv, man!' Mum's still at the door, listening.

'The Shelbourne. He said I was good looking and gave me ten pounds.'

'Dirty bastard! Next time you call the guards. Christ!' says Lucy.

Now something really peculiar happens. Emma stares at Mum with a look that would skin a rabbit. 'This time, sadly, I don't think the police are necessary. Are they, *Mother*?'

Mum stares daggers back at Emma. 'I never knew you could be so disloyal.'

'Dear pot, love kettle,' replies Emma.

'Have you any idea what it was like to go through the war? Have you any concept what it cost me to bring you and your two siblings into the world? The pain of childbirth? Wait until you try, *Saint* Emma!' Mum is on a furious roll and leaves, slamming the door.

Lucy's outraged and amused at the same time. 'I love that. Pops us out like farts and hands us straight to nannies. Bloody martyr! She thinks a nappy's a new kind of cocktail.'

Now we're all laughing and I think it's the perfect time for my new joke, the one Annie just told me. 'Hey, what was the guard doing up the tree?'

'Go on,' says Lucy.

'Looking for the *Special Branch*.'

'That's years old, man.'

'Sorry, *man*.'

'But Justin, how did you meet him?' asks the oldest sister, all suspicious.

'Who?'

'The pervert.'

'He knew Annie.'

'Annie?' Says Lucy. 'You were with Annie? Jesus!'

'You're crazy, man. The old man'll kill you,' says Lucy.

'We were in the Lord Mayor's Lounge, having tea.'

'What did he look like?'

'English. Yeah, and he was called …'

'Roger?' asks Emma. I'm too surprised to speak.

*

Helen enters the study but Bobby doesn't look up. He continues watching the news on the two televisions while holding up the cigarette case, waiting for Helen to take it. 'It's not what you think,' she says to his unmoving back.

'What does it matter?'

'It matters to me. I didn't want to have to tell you. After all, Bobby, I created the problem, not you. He wants to see his son. That's why I went to meet him.' Helen pauses. 'He said if I didn't, he'd come to The Hall, find Justin, and introduce himself.'

'He what? I don't believe it. Is he mad? Are you telling the truth? I'm coming to the end of my tether, Helen. I really am. I'm not going to just stand by and watch …'

'About bloody time,' whispers Helen under her breath.

'What did you say?'

'Nothing.' Helen feels there has been enough emotion expressed and sits down in the armchair next to Bobby's. She speaks gently, in a voice that always gets her what she wants. 'Bobby? I'd love one of your special martinis. Would you mind terribly? Please?'

'Get one yourself. I'm not your blasted butler, thank you very bloody much.'

Autumn

Fourteen

I've never let my school interfere with my education.

Mark Twain

Thursday, 5 September 1963

We're on the way down the avenue, Emma and Lucy and me. The Aer Fungus Viscount doesn't leave for another three hours. But by the time Donal gets us to Dublin airport, it could be bloody midnight. I hate leaving home even when the old man is in residence, but I love going on the plane. This time we're going First Class, thank God. I am sure the old man only puts us in First because he feels guilty packing us off to school in England.

As the Jag bumps gently over the large potholes, I stare out at the Liffey running alongside the road and I think back to just a few months ago when the weather went totally wild and our land turned to water. Last winter was the most savage Ireland had seen for 200 years. It began freezing on Christmas Day and didn't really thaw until March. From Boxing Day onwards the old man was very busy as there were all sorts of problems on the farm: animals dying, pipes freezing and bursting, staff sick and not able to come to work. Worst of all for him, he couldn't get to Dublin to go to the cinema. I think he was suffering from severe John Wayne withdrawal. I didn't give a hoot and absolutely loved it. The snow was so high it was incredible.

Finally, after three weeks of misery and an awful lot of moaning, the old man ordered one of the lads, Jimmy Duffy, to use a tractor with a front loader to shift the massive piles of snow. It took three days to push a clear path all of two miles up to the main road. Then we got the Jag out and drove all the way to Dublin to go to the Russell and then to the cinema. On the way we passed loads of vehicles, especially trucks, just abandoned in the ditches.

It took about four hours, this journey, as we kept getting stuck and sliding into drifts. When we finally got there we made a brief stop at Smith's of the Green. We were late for lunch at the Russell so the old man, having parked the Jag outside Smith's with the engine running, asked me to sprint in and get two magnums of Mum's special champagne, Krug 1953, and put it on his account. When I politely asked for the two magnums and stated my name, the staff hesitated. I had wet trousers up to my knees and was now filthy from having helped to push the car when we got stuck. The staff called for the snooty manager, who appeared, full of grandeur in his morning coat, and asked for some form of identification as he 'couldn't just hand over the most expensive Krug' to someone he didn't recognize. Oh dear me, no.

I wasn't used to people questioning who I was. I mean, Ireland is a small place and I thought everyone knew who we were. So I just said: 'Sorry, I don't have any identification. I'm twelve years old.'

'I am sorry too, young man. Smith's of the Green could not possibly just release two bottles of their finest without knowing who you are. Especially as you are, if you don't mind me saying, wearing such a strange get-up.'

Oh for fuck's sake. At this point all the people in the shop were staring at me like I was a Dublin gurrier. On top of this, I was also getting worried as the old man was now hooting the horn and would kill me if I didn't come out with the bubbles. Just at that moment I had one of my brilliant ideas. I dropped my trousers and turned around and pulled back the top half of my underpants to show the stupid manager my school name tag: *J.A.T.E.P. Montague.*

After the initial embarrassment the manager decided to accept my ID and send me on my way as fast as possible, clutching the two incredibly expensive magnums of Krug.

The Aer Lingus air hostess, Dolores, who is totally gorgeous, has given me a smoked salmon sandwich and keeps stroking my hair. The propellers have just started but I can't hear what she's saying because of the terrible racket and I don't care because I am not listening, just staring. She has bigger bubbly doops than Bridget and she can lean as close as she likes, thinking she's being motherly. Personally I'm getting a little excited but as I have a First-Class blanket over my knees there is no way she can tell. Otherwise, I'd probably be getting a whack around the head instead.

I stare out the oval windows of the Aer Lingus Viscount and try to distract myself from the Aer Lingus breasts by watching the hares bouncing around on the grass. Dublin Airport has always had an invasion of huge hares. My first nanny, Sissy, used to tell us how they were 'making Marmite', but now I'm a little older I'm not sure I believe her. We're off now, flying away and turning out over Dublin Bay, heading towards bloody England and bloody school.

Back home during that terrible spell last winter, me, Annie and the local lads built snowmen and had snowball fights. I mean, sure, it was freezing cold, but the winters in Ireland were never exactly warm so it didn't really bother us. Even at The Hall we didn't have central heating, just fires in all the main rooms. Of course we didn't use coal like the English. We used turf, cut from the Wicklow Mountains, and we had a huge store full.

This turf was cut by the lads from our very own patch, then transported down to the yard on a tractor and trailer and piled up in the turf shed. Afterwards, Jack Cully, an old IRA man whose job it was to polish and bone all the hunting boots and make sure all the fires were laid and the stoves lit, would use a wheelbarrow to bring the turf into the entrance hall and fill the turf basket. Then it was the job of all the dogs in the house to fetch the pieces of turf into whichever room needed it.

Generally we had lots of dogs at The Hall. But when Cromwell arrived, he ruled the roost and the other dogs, labradors and Jack Russell terriers, were never replaced when they died because Cromwell wouldn't allow it. So before the reign of Cromwell, the old man had all the labs and Jack Russells trained up. Having noticed that a fire in a certain room needed more fuel he would let out a huge roar: 'Turf! Turf! Turf!'

All the dogs would immediately fly into the entrance hall yapping away with excitement, skidding round the corners and leap into the turf basket. They would then grab a piece of turf in their mouths and rush back into the old man, wagging their tails at how clever they were. The problem for the terriers was that sometimes the turf would be too big and they would get stuck trying to get a long piece round a bend or through a door. Sometimes they ended up dragging a piece round and round in circles because it was too heavy and they just couldn't carry it. There was no way they were going to let go, because they were terriers after all.

When I was born there was a very sweet, bristly little Jack Russell terrier who came from the local vicar. He was only a year older than me and didn't really show much interest in anyone until I appeared on the scene. For some reason, Boozer, as he was called, decided he belonged to me. Or more likely, I belonged to him. (Boozer was so named because he was always licking the tops of empty beer bottles when he was a puppy.) Anyway, Boozer decided that we belonged to each other and would snarl at anyone who came too close to my cot when I was a baby. He would stand guard and was finally allowed to sleep in the nursery.

When I got a little bigger, Boozer and I had a really good time together, although he could easily become distracted. Boozer could smell sex miles away and whenever he disappeared for a couple of days nobody was worried. We all knew what he was up to. Eventually Boozer would stagger back towards The Hall, shagged out, and weighing about five pounds less. Having been let in again he would slump down in front of the fireplace, generally in the study, and fall fast asleep for about twenty-four hours. You could put a raw steak or even an open box of Laura Secord chocolates right in front of his nose and he wouldn't even blink, I swear to God.

Boozer was very faithful. Once I had a row with Mum. It wasn't really her fault: I'd put a banger in her cigarette and she was none too pleased. It was early evening and we were alone in the drawing room with Boozer. After her gold Cocktail Sobranie exploded, Mum leapt up off the sofa and tried to belt me. I grabbed her wrists and held firm so that she couldn't. At that point Boozer leaps up himself and starts to snarl, really angry. Mum was delighted. She reckoned that Boozer was going to bite me because she was always feeding the dogs titbits so they would love her more than anyone else.

So Mum shouts out all triumphant:

'Now you'll pay, you dreadful little brat!'

But Boozer had other ideas – after a moment's pause for some major Jack Russell decision-making, he bounded across the floor and seized hold of Mum's left ankle. Boozer didn't really sink his teeth in because he wasn't a vicious dog, but Mum was devastated by his disloyalty and refused to feed him chocolates ever again. I don't think Boozer really cared. He was much more interested in having sex.

When I was younger and the old man turned on me, I used to get upset and I wouldn't know what to do. Whenever I tried to talk to someone, anyone, I would generally get the same bloody answer. 'Ah now, don't worry your father.'

I had no one to turn to. I had to do something. Eventually I figured out a solution: I would talk to Boozer. I used to lie down on the lawn and pour my heart out to him and although I don't think he understood, he was a damn sight better listener than everyone bloody else. I think he stopped me from going totally mad.

It was horrible when Boozer died but I am glad I was there when it happened. I came home last Christmas holidays, just before the big freeze had set in. Poor old Boozer had become so old he was nearly blind and totally deaf and no longer recognized me. It was hard for me to look at him as I was really choked. When I went up and stroked him, he suddenly got excited and jumped up and down as much as he could. He must have recognized my smell.

On Christmas Day, we woke to find the ground covered in a blanket of snow higher than anyone had ever seen it.

You could not see any green whatsoever, anywhere. Bridget appeared at breakfast full of tears and asked me to go with her into one of the greenhouses. I was stunned. There was the body of poor old Boozer laid out on a bench, stiff as a board. Liam had been driving back from midnight Mass on Christmas Eve through the first blizzard and Boozer, totally blind and deaf as he was, had walked out under the Jaguar that Liam had borrowed for the evening. Bridget said that Liam was very upset and asked me if I wouldn't mind going up and telling him it wasn't his fault. So I dried my tears as best as I could and went up to see Liam and told him I didn't blame him. I am a good actor if needs must. When I was giving Liam the little speech and even though I was smiling sympathetically, I wanted to kill him for murdering my friend, even though I knew it wasn't his fault.

The big thaw didn't happen until the end of March. By the time we arrived back from school, the vast amounts of snow had melted. We couldn't understand why a taxi had been sent to pick us up from the airport and deliver us home, but we realized very quickly when we arrived at the main gates to The Hall. There was an old rowing boat to meet us with Liam in charge. It was one of the lifeboats, a tender, from our yacht, the *Diana*. We loaded all our suitcases into the rowing boat, put on some life jackets and off we went. As Liam set a course for the house I strained my eyes but I couldn't spot the avenue itself. It had disappeared. The Liffey had flooded its banks and it was just water, water, water, as far as the eye could see.

For the next couple of weeks the lads who lived past the main gates away from the estate, had to come to work by boat. One day while we were still at school there was a bit of a swell on the water because of the wind, and poor old Paddy Kelly got seasick. Another time apparently, the old man got very emotional because one of his dirty Friesian cows was swept away down the river. At least it was clean when it died.

Winter

Fifteen

A child miseducated is a child lost.
John F. Kennedy

Saturday, 16 November 1963

I stare with disgust at the sign on the wall: '*Hampshire House School for Young Gentlemen.*' Beside it is the postbox. I kiss the envelope for luck and slip it through the opening.

I don't like it here at school in England. First, I am away from all my friends. And second, I am bored. The old man has always told me that I am stupid and will never get to Oxford like him and I should concentrate on sports instead. So that's what I do, and I'm not half bad at running probably because I spent a childhood drinking Lucozade and flying round the garden like Ronnie.

Here comes good old stuttering George, Hampshire's most miserable postman, arriving dead on time to deliver the school post. Please God, let him have a letter for me. And not the usual monthly newsletter from the old man, although they're quite entertaining, I hate to admit. I want one, just one single letter from Annie. I haven't had any for ages, which is just not like her and makes me sad.

The newsletters from the old man to Lucy and Emma, who are at a convent in Ascot near the racecourse, surprise,

surprise, and the newsletter to myself, are exactly the same. The old man types the letter, copying it three times. The only difference between them is that he writes the *Dear Justin* and the *Love Dad* in his own hand.

The Hall,
Rathpeader,
Near Kilcullen,
County Kildare,
Telephone: Kilcullen 211.

Dear Justin,

I hope you are well and working hard. You had better do as your mother and I have spent a fortune on your educations, I'll have you know. And the fees have gone up again.

Things here at The Hall are good all round, although the weather is lousy, as per bloody usual. Christ, if it wasn't for the cheap taxes, your mother and I would go back and live in England near your stuck-up relations. At least we'd have some efficient services. Talking of services, Andy the postman has just been given a van to replace his bicycle. Pity he hasn't got a bloody driving license. Jesus, what is this country coming to?

And talking of taxes, I had an inspector down here the other day, a junior one at that, and can you credit it, he turned up without an appointment. Cheeky sod! I told him to go back to his office and not to come back until he had one. Guess what? He refused to leave until he'd had a look at my books. Well, that was the end of that, I can tell you. I told him he could bugger off my land, otherwise he'd end up in the Liffey like the last inspector I had a run-in with. He was off like a scared rabbit, double bloody quick!

Night Train runs next week at Navan in a three-mile handicap hurdle. He has a very good chance as he's well in at the weight if that idiotic jockey, Brennan, doesn't get a fit of the slows. I am a little worried about Brennan. I'm not sure his nerves are holding.

Talking of nerves, your mother has bought me this enormous grey horse as a birthday present. He's called Gandalf. There he was, Gandalf, on my very birthday, standing in the yard with a huge red ribbon round his neck. I would never have bought him, not in a million years. He's got a wild eye, and if you know anything about horses, you'd only have to take one look at him to realize you shouldn't buy him. Maybe she does know and she's trying to kill me? Ha ha.

Anyway all the lads were watching, so I had to get on him, otherwise I'd look like a complete coward. And boy, was I right about the wild eye. He's a nutter. He tried to scrape me off straight away by backing against the milking-shed door. But what can I do? Your mother, bless her, has obviously made such an effort to find him and I cannot let her down, so I am taking him hunting next Wednesday at Dunlavin. Luckily, I have had a terrific idea which will sort him out before the meet starts. Danny Keogh is going to trot Gandalf to Dunlavin, all of fifteen miles. 'That'll learn him' as they say in this part of the world. Gandalf will be banjaxed by the time I get on him, and hopefully he'll have learned his lesson. And if he hasn't, I'll get Danny to trot him all the way back.

Anyway, we're off to Dublin just now, lunch at the Russell, then a movie – Call Me Bwana, *starring Bob Hope.*

Cromwell is on flying form you'll be pleased to hear, although he was in trouble last week with a local farmer, Liam Heggarty. Cromwell decided that Heggarty's sheep looked tasty and killed two of them. Greedy bugger! Heggarty, of course, charged me double price for damages. Bloody money-grabbing Irish, as usual. You can't trust them, can you?

Love from your mother,
Dad

PS *Good news! Some lads from the council have been tarmacking the road outside the main gates. I've had a word and asked if they'd like to earn a few extra bob at the weekend. They said yes instantly. They're not stupid. Next Saturday they are going to bring the steamroller and tarmac machine up the avenue into the garden and lay us a tennis court. What do you think of that? In the strawberry beds. All-weather no less, and easy to keep. Get practising!*

PPS *That mad Macdonald from up the road came here the other day with his two daughters. They should be well ready to lose their virginity by now, after all that riding to meets. Hah!*

Mad Macdonald lived near to us and had two cute daughters and loads of money. But he would never buy a horse box, even though some of the hunt meets he went to were over twenty miles away. As a result Macdonald and his daughters used to ride all they way to the meets. The old man once asked him why he didn't buy a box? Macdonald had a simple answer. 'When my daughters get married I want them well ready for it. If they get to trot their horses miles and miles to every meet that'll help. They'll be all prepared, so to speak, with the long hours spent in the saddle.'

'For what?' asked the old man, somehow realizing he already knew the answer but hoping he didn't.

'For the marriage bed, Bobby. So they're nicely opened up and it won't hurt them!'

*

Bobby Montague is at his desk, having just finished the monthly letter to the children. He is now wondering if he can come up with a brilliant scheme to make some serious money out of his wife's fortune, to prove to her family trustees that he is a super-smooth businessman and not the hillbilly they have always thought him to be. Bobby stares out the window. He is easily distracted.

Outside, Gandalf trot-canters past, mostly sideways, being ridden by Danny Keogh, who looks terrified. Donal drives into the yard in the Jaguar and Annie Cassidy, carrying an envelope, appears at the same time.

As Donal gets out of the car, Annie greets him, cheeky as usual. 'Good morning, Mr Sheridan,' says Annie.

'You're a bold girl, Annie Cassidy. And what are up to? Some kind of mischief, no doubt.'

'If you must know, Mr Sheridan, I'm posting a letter to the man I'm going to marry – Master Justin Alexander Torquhil Edward Peregrine Montague.'

'I warned you, you little brat! Stay away from him.'

Annie trots off, laughing. 'It's my party and I'll cry if I want to, cry if I want to ...'

Donal is livid. But a wicked smile spreads across his face. He makes a decision. He removes his hat, replaces the smile with a forced frown, and strides purposefully towards the house.

Bobby watches as Annie goes to the estate letterbox on the wall, kisses the envelope and tries to slip it into the slot. Clumsy as usual, she drops the letter instead. Laughing, she picks it up and pops it into the box.

Bobby, shaking his head at the stupidity of the girl, goes back to his thoughts. Moments later, there is a knock on the study door. Bobby is grateful for the interruption. 'Come in!' he booms.

Donal walks in. 'Good morning, sir.'

'It is a good morning Donal, and lovely and quiet without that bloody idiot Justin running around, driving me mad.'

'Well, sir. It's Justin I wanted to talk to you about, sir.'

'Justin's at school in England.'

'It's about what was going on behind your back, sir, before he left and even now, that is. It's more than my job's worth, sir.'

'What the bloody hell are you blathering on about?' Bobby is frustrated. He can never understand why the Irish don't just get straight to the point.

Minutes later, steaming with indignation, Bobby strides across the yard. 'Jesus, bloody Christ, that little fucker! You've had it this time. Oh yes, you fucking have!'

He knows in his heart that aside from killing Justin, there is nothing much he can do. If he takes his anger out on Helen, she'll leave him: and if he doesn't do something, he'll just explode.

Bobby unlocks the letterbox, rummages around and pulls out an envelope.

'Think I'm stupid? We'll soon see about that, you little cunt!' Tearing up the envelope as he walks to the back door, he drops the pieces in an outside bin, walks in, and slams the door behind him.

*

It's breakfast in St James' House and there's silence until we're given permission to speak. Me and Norton II, the youngest of the snotty English boys, have to serve as it's our first year in the big school. Our fat kinky housemaster, Mr Macadam, wearing shorts and long yellow shooting socks with brown garters, sits at top table. Now he rises, holding the post, and I'm watching him, really hoping for a letter. Please God let me have one, just one, and I won't ask again. And now he's calling out the names, and the boys are going up for to get their letters.

'Calthorpe. Buckley. Chumley-Watson. Hesketh II. Vaughan. Williams. Norton I. Tempest.'

Then he stops and sits back down. Oh no, that's it. I know it.

'You may speak!' shouts Mr Macadam and a huge chatter erupts all around. Speaking is the last thing I want to do. I'm feeling so sad and I just want to go home. People often say to me that I must love it at school in England because I can escape the wrath of the old man, but it's not true: I'd rather be at home as he's not always bad, especially when I get things right. Sometimes the parentals go off on holiday and then everything's perfect and we can have the run of The Hall, which is brilliant.

I can't eat and I'm not allowed Lucozade and I just wish

I had the nerve to run away and disappear to Spain or some-where hot. That fat spotty git, Adams, with his stuck-up Eng-lish voice, is staring hard and I know he's going to have a go.

'*Hey*, Montague?' he says, really, really loud and now everyone's watching. 'No letters, poor thing? Although, come to think of it, can anyone in Ireland actually write? Rumour has it Oliver Cromwell burnt all the bog men with brains. Not that it was a very big fire, was it?'

And now they're all laughing at me.

I remember the first time I arrived here in England. My school then was called Junior House and it was the prepa-ratory school for Hampshire House School. All the boys at Junior House were really young, between seven and thirteen, at which stage you took your Common Entrance and moved into the big school, presuming you passed, that is. The old man had decided that I should start a little earlier at the age of six as it would 'sort you out and stop you being so wild'.

A chauffeur in a black Daimler from a firm called Gor-don Jacks met us at Heathrow Airport and I was definitely quite excited as we drove through the airport tunnel past all the orange lights. The bit I didn't like was when we pulled up at the school.

'All right, old cock. Don't forget to write to your mother,' said the old man, all cheery, pleased to be rid of me. 'And don't forget to let your grandmother know when you get a weekend break. If she's not too busy she'll have you to stay. She'll probably let you even bring a friend if you play your cards right.' (Charlton was the next-door estate.)

So I reached up to kiss him goodbye but he backed off like he'd been shot. He just grabbed my hand and shook it, very manly.

'You're a bit too old for all that stuff, Justin. All right, off you go now. Don't stand gawping.'

He jumped back in the car and they drove off. There I was left alone standing on the crunchy gravel beside my bags, watching the Daimler disappear down the drive. I knew my parents weren't great but I never imagined they could just dump me here by myself. What had I done wrong?

Our dormitory was enormous: a huge octagonal room on the first floor. There were about twenty beds. On the first night, Fanshawe, the dormitory monitor, who had already been there a couple of terms, told us what to do. 'Right! Lights out, you little shits. No more talking.'

We all curled up and tried to sleep but it was only 8:30 and the sun was still pouring through the windows and all I could think of was everyone at home out playing by the Liffey or on the farm while I was stuck here in bed in a weird place in the middle of nowhere. I had never felt so much loneliness before.

I lay there that first summer's night trying really hard not to cry. A few beds away I could hear another new boy, Evans-Williams, sobbing away, poor fella. Fanshawe was not impressed and shouted at him to be quiet.

'Stop your snivelling or you'll go on report!' Evans-Williams didn't stop as he couldn't stop and the very next day he received three of the best from the headmaster. Three of the best meant three whacks on the bare bum from a huge white gym shoe.

The headmaster of Junior House was called Jocelyn Trubbs-Laycock and he was quite old by the time I arrived. He never really spoke to me and I don't think he taught me anything. He was just in charge. I do remember Sundays, though. On Sundays we could wear either our family kilt, or boy scout's uniform if you had passed all the tests to be one. I couldn't believe my eyes when Mr Trubbs-Laycock appeared for Church wearing full boy scout's uniform, whistle, shorts, the lot. He looked hysterical because he was fat, very bald, and nearly sixty-five years old. No one dared laugh as we were all so afraid of him and his gym shoe.

That summer of 1956, my first term, I was beaten twice. I don't know why, I swear to God. For some reason I just can't remember what he told me as he pulled down my shorts. I do remember it hurt but I didn't cry. I just prayed really, really hard to God, to kill him.

As a special treat every Saturday night we had a film-screening in this huge room. It was normally a war picture showing all these heroic British soldiers winning battles, like *Reach for the Sky* about the fighter pilot Douglas Bader who lost his legs in the war. On the first day back for the next term that autumn of 1956, we had a showing of a film called *Whiskey Galore*.

Before the film started, the sports teacher, Mr Needham, appeared and told us all the 'terrible news that your beloved headmaster, Jocelyn Trubbs-Laycock, has passed away during your school holidays'.

I didn't dare tell anyone that it might have been me who'd had him killed.

Sixteen

*One should not lose one's temper, unless
one is certain of getting more and more
angry to the end.*

William Butler Yeats

Saturday, 16 November 1963

*Halfway up the avenue, Liam Cassidy is painting a black
five-bar gate that leads into the lawn field, a huge piece
of land where the horses are often galloped as the ground
always manages to stay good, even when it's been raining.
Maureen Cassidy appears with a thermos and a packet of
chicken sandwiches. She loves surprising her husband.*

*The Jaguar rolls down the avenue towards the main gates.
Bobby is driving. He is dressed in hunting green, the correct
attire for hare-hunting. Helen sits beside him, clasping his
huge Zeiss binoculars, wearing tweeds but still managing to
look elegant. On the red leather rear seat sits Bobby's hunting hat and crop, a full picnic basket and Cromwell.*

'It's so quiet without the children now they're back at
school,' says Helen. 'Is that an awful thing to say?'

'I miss the noise, sometimes.'

'Do you really?'

'Yes. Apart from the boy. I know it's not his fault, but

it's his face. It's such a reminder.' Bobby is determined to
remain firm.

'I know, darling. I know. I'm sorry. I really am.' She
rubs the side of his huge arm with fondness.

'Here we go!' says Bobby as he stops the Jaguar beside
Liam and Maureen sitting on the grass verge, eating sandwiches and supping tea. The Cassidys put down their cups
and stand up. Liam doffs his cap.

'Morning, boss. M'lady.'

'M'lady,' adds Maureen respectfully, and bowing slightly.

'Good morning,' says Helen.

'So, what are you working at today, Liam?'

'Em, after this? Digging the new strawberry patch. It's a
shambles, boss. An absolute shambles.'

'Right, forget the strawberry patch. Do it tomorrow.'

'Right boss.'

'Grab a tractor and go up and plough the field, the one
behind the haggard.'

'Which one, boss?'

'Which one? Which one?' Bobby explodes. 'Oh for
Christ's sake, the one we always plough. Can't you think for
your bloody self, Cassidy? Jesus bloody Christ!'

Bobby drives off at high speed, looking thunderous,
leaving Liam and Maureen in his wake. They are stunned:
he's often angry, the boss man, but never for no reason.
Apart from anything else, if he is angry with the staff, it is
never, ever, with Liam.

As soon as he is out of sight of the Cassidys, Bobby
relaxes, and a wide smirk spreads across his face. 'What are
you so pleased about?' asks Helen.

'Hey? Oh nothing. A private joke.'

We're sitting in the classroom waiting for the teacher and I'm hungry as I haven't eaten but I'm not sure what the first class is so I ask.

'What's first, lads?' Oh feck it! Me and my big mouth. Adams, that fat git and class bully, can't resist.

'Lads? *Lads?* History, you stupid Irish bog man!' Everyone laughs. Not because he's amusing but because they're all afraid of him as he's bloody strong and whacks anyone who upsets him. I don't care any more as I haven't had a letter from Annie and I'll fight him to the death if I have to, even if he thinks I'm only a skinny little Irish runt.

'I'll get you later Adams – you fat, spotty, toffee-nosed English twat!' says I, surprising myself and everyone else with my bravery.

Jesus bloody Christ, you could have heard a pencil drop. Adams looks as taken aback as the rest of those Anglo-Saxon wankers. But pride's at stake and he pulls himself together and jumps up to come and get me. 'You fucking potato-muncher! I'm going to beat you to …'

'*Sit down!*' I'm saved by the skin of my teeth as the history master Mr Brown enters the room. Silence. I watch him as he performs his normal ritual of placing his umbrella under his desk and a wicker basket on top with *The Times*, as usual, sticking out the side. I bet he never reads it. It's just for show. Then he does something he's never done before, and puts his right hand on his right hip and sort of leans back and addresses the whole world but not one person in particular, all in his special fake-aristocratic drawl.

'The naked human body is the most *beauuutiful* thing in the whole world!' Now we're all united, us boys, scratching our arses and wondering what the fuck he's on about and I've just had enough of England and the bloody English for one day and I know I shouldn't do it but I can't help it.

'Excuse me, sir?'

'Ah Montague, with that *rather* trying Irish accent. Speak!'

I can hear Adams chortling away behind me.

'How long have you been teaching history, you fecking English pervert?'

*

At The Hall, in a field behind the haggard, Liam Cassidy sits on a noisy, shaky Massey Ferguson tractor, ploughing. Why, he thinks to himself, did he ask me to plough this stupid field? It doesn't make sense. But then, nothing the boss man does makes sense.

*

I'm bending over and there's only two more whacks to go and my arse is stinging but it was worth all ten with the enormous gym shoe belonging by that pervert of a house master, Mr Macadam. I stand up slowly, rubbing my sore behind. My arse may be red but I will not, absolutely not, let him see any change in my face. 'I apologize for my behaviour, sir. It will not happen again,' he says, panting and out of breath. Not only has he flayed me alive, he's now teaching me what to say.

He is a little deaf so I'll make the most of it.

'I apologize for my behaviour, sir, calling Mr Brown a pervert, which he is. It will not happen again,' says I, softly.

'What? What did you say?'

'Nothing sir,' says I, all innocent. 'Just what you said.'
'Get out! *Out!*'

*

It is mid-afternoon. The field behind the haggard is finished, beautifully ploughed. Liam Cassidy leans over a gate, admiring the straight lines. 'Ah well, that's what the man wanted and he pays the wages.'

In Lady Helen's bedroom, three Chanel evening dresses are laid out on the bed. Annie is standing in front of the dressing-mirror in a beautiful blue and gold ball gown. She talks to herself in a grand English voice. 'The first dance? Of course, Sir Percy. Shall we?' Annie swirls, spinning round in high heels.

As she spins, she hears a car coming down the avenue.

Inside the Jaguar, Helen is confused. 'You still haven't explained why you stopped so early. It was such a good day and the scent was so strong, I thought the hounds would go on for ever.'

Bobby's face is criss-crossed with bloody thorn scratches – heroic, manly scars from the hunting field.

'Hey?' Bobby, distracted, peers through his windscreen. Without warning, he shoves his right hunting boot on the brake and stops the car so fast that Cromwell falls off the back seat.

'What now?' asks Helen, growing impatient with her husband's increasingly peculiar behaviour.

Ignoring his wife, Bobby grabs his binoculars, jumps out, and stands looking into the distance. Through the 7 x 50 lens, even though it is almost dark, he can just make out the beautifully ploughed field. Bobby smiles and gets back into the car.

'Darling, whatever's the matter with you? You're behaving very queerly!'

Bobby doesn't answer. He's far too excited about what's about to happen.

Minutes later, the newly lit turf fire blazes in Bobby's study. Cromwell, lying by the fire, snarls. Bobby is sitting on the black leather and brass fender and removing one of his hunting boots with a boot-jack.

'Would you like to explain how, on God's earth, you managed to plough the wrong field?'

Liam Cassidy stands almost to attention, very wary, cap in hand. 'I didn't, boss. That's the one you told me to.'

'No, it bloody wasn't! Do you like working here?'

Liam is frozen with fear. Fear of giving the wrong answer, fear of losing his job.

'I said, do you like working here?'

Lady Helen walks into her bedroom and stops in her tracks. She cannot believe her eyes. 'What on earth do you think you are doing?'

Back in Bobby's study, Liam is trying to stop himself from getting deeper into trouble.

'The best job around, sir.'

Bobby's boot comes off with a pop. He waves the boot hook at Liam.

'The only job around. I'll tell you something, Cassidy, you're not wasting my good money. So, in your own good time, with your own bare hands, you will turn back the sod. Every single piece. The whole field. Tomorrow!'

'But it's Sunday, sir, tomorrow, it is. My only day with the family.'

'I don't give a tinker's cuss,' says Bobby.

Liam looks upset, but he is relieved. At least it's over, he thinks. I still have my job, thank the Lord.

Bobby is delighted with the execution of his plan. At the same time, he knows he will not be happy to see Liam go: Liam Arthur Cassidy, unlike the rest of the bloody Irish nation, is a great worker. It will take at least two men to replace him. Luckily, farm labour is cheap. Liam will just have to be sacrificed.

Seventeen

I am a Christian. That obliges me to be a Communist.

George Bernard Shaw

Sunday, 17 November 1963

It's ten in the morning and it's wet. In the middle of the ploughed field stands Liam Cassidy, pouring with sweat, drenched with rainwater and replacing sods of earth. Bobby stands looking over the gate, watching. He is dressed for Mass, a Bible in his hand.

'Ya big bully!' *Annie shouts at Bobby from behind.*

'Annie!' *Maureen is horrified at her daughter's outburst.*

Bobby, straightening his face into a terrible scowl, whips around to confront Maureen and Annie. 'You want to control your daughter, Maureen Cassidy. Not only has she a big mouth, but my wife caught her sneaking around in my house, in our own fecking bedroom, wearing my wife's best clothes. Unbelievable!'

'Yes sir. I heard. I'm very sorry, sir. I'll have a word,' *says Maureen.*

'You do that. Otherwise, she'll end up on the street, like so many of her type.'

Maureen cannot believe her ears. 'What did you say?'

'I said: she'll end up on the street, like so many of her type.'

Maureen shouts across the field at her husband. 'Liam? Time for Mass. Come on. Now!'

Bobby pretends outrage. 'Hang fire! I didn't give him permission.'

'You don't have to give him bloody permission, because you can stick your job up your you-know-where,' says Maureen, angrier than she's ever been in her life. 'You think you're clever just because you married money. Well, you're not. You're nothing but a big gombeen!'

Maureen storms past Bobby, through the gate, into the field, and up to Liam. Meanwhile, Annie cannot resist having another go at Bobby. She's always hated him and now's her chance to have a real dig.

'Hey Mister? How come a horrible person like you managed to have such a great son?'

'Ah, there's the rub: maybe I didn't. Don't forget Mass now,' says Bobby cheerfully.

Eighteen

Lack of money is the root of all evil.
George Bernard Shaw

Thursday, 21 November 1963
It's night at school. Everyone's asleep and I've sneaked through the dark corridors and now I'm in the phone box. I've got Mum on the blower and she sounds sober, which is strange for eleven o'clock at night. 'Mum? Can you hear me? I wanted to ask you ...'

*

The Montagues are in bed. Cromwell lies between them, snoring happily. Bobby pretends to read his Horse And Hound *while listening with great interest to Helen's phone call.*

Helen continues without pause. 'Very well, thank you darling. Although, it's a frightfully bad line. Anyway, Night Train runs next week at Fairyhouse. He should win ...'

'As long as that arse of a jockey doesn't fall off like last time,' interrupts Bobby.

'Oh, and I ordered a stunning gown from Sybill for the Kilcullen Hunt Ball. I do hope it's not full of trogs like last year.

*Oh yes, your poor father is very upset. Liam's wife ...' She
hesitates and turns to Bobby. 'What is her name, darling?'*

'Maureen,' answers Bobby.

*'Anyway Justin, Maureen Cassidy was frightfully rude,
and then Liam literally gave his notice, which is very unwise.
Where's he going to find work or a home for that matter?
Justin? Are you there? Hello? ...'*

*Why has Justin put the phone down? She doesn't believe
she has been cut off.*

*Bobby watches Helen carefully as she processes these
thoughts. And in a moment of bravery, inspired by the fact
that everything is going as planned, the way he wants it for
once in his bloody life, Bobby grabs Helen, roughly.*

'Come here! Now, I said, you bitch!'

*Helen is speechless. Cromwell, startled, is kicked flying
off the bed by his lord and master.*

*Bobby is giving Helen, for the first time in years, what
she has always wanted.*

*

It's like I'm in a dream and I'm looking at my feet then I'm
looking down at the ground way below me and I know if I
jump I'll make a terrible splatter in the courtyard. I hope they
make that fat wanker Adams sweep me up, all the bloody
mess. I wish I was there to see it. So, Dad, you win. Sound
man. Fair play to ya.

I look up at the stars, twinkling away they are, and it's
my favourite time of day, night-time is, and the sky's all clear
but I'm still going to jump all the way down from the school
roof exactly ninety-seven-and-a-half feet according to Callaghan, the maths master, and it's a perfect evening to do it. I
hope to fuck there's a heaven otherwise I'm in big shit.

He was a right eeiit, that Callaghan. He used to teach biology as well as maths and once he got a hold of these two South American toads, Romeo and Juliet he called them, even if he wasn't really sure of their sex. He kept them for us to gawp at in a special temperature-controlled fish tank. God, it was the latest thing this contraption and Callagasbags, as we called him, was really proud of it. One night there was a power cut all over Hampshire and when they put it back on, the thermostat switches went wrong on the fish tank. When we got in for first class there was poor old Callaghan, sentimental fucker, in floods of tears over his toads, who'd been boiled alive.

So here I am about to take the final leap when I hear this bloody song and I can't get it out of my head. '*It's my party and I'll cry if I want to, cry if I want to, cry if I want to. You would cry too, if it happened to you.*' Bloody disloyal bitch who hasn't even bothered to write me a fecking letter. She's still in my bloody head.

'Oh bollocks. Fuck everybody. *Fuck the lot of ya!*' I am going to jump. That's it. Fuck you all – Annie, the old man, Mum, even the sisters and all those other bloody people who just wouldn't listen, like fat old Cook, trying to keep the peace just so as she doesn't get yelled at herself.

'*Ah now, don't worry the boss, me little gossoon.*'

Or Bridget trying to keep me from cracking up by making him seem nicer than he really is.

'*He's not that bad, really, your dad. He shouts and roars but then he forgets it in no time.*'

Or Mum, telling the biggest lie of all.

'*I know he shouts sometimes, but it means nothing, darling. He adores you.*'

They'll all be sorry and I hope they feel really, really guilty. And if they give me a funeral everyone will be staring at the old man like it's his fault and you won't know where to look, will you, you arse? Now I am really thinking again and changing tack. Fuck him! What about me? What about Justin? What if I do jump and die? What if there's no Heaven? What if it's like out there in space, going on forever, nothing but darkness? What if nobody cares anyway? What's the alternative? Stand up to him? How can I stand up to him, how can I possibly beat him? I'm only small and a weed and he's huge and hairy and full of hate. Christ alive, I don't think I have ever felt this angry in my whole life.

But then something strange happens. I feel the energy leave me and I sit down on the wall and I start to cry. Not crying like when Boozer died, or even Grandpa Charlton – this is more like the dam bursting at Poulaphouca. So I just sit there for at least ten whole minutes while the floodgates open until I cannot cry any more and my left ear is blocked from all the sobbing. The weird thing is, at the end of the crying when I am dried out and nothing more will come, I feel a little better, I swear to God. Probably better than I have for years. And on top of that, the feeling better, I'm very, very focused as I know for the first time in my life exactly what I have to do. Oh yes, *exactly*. So I take the big leap and jump down, not into the school yard, but back down onto the roof top and away from the parapet.

I'm striding through the dormitory like a ghost and I feel like I'm floating and I am so focused that I don't care about what I see out of the corner of my right eye. That fat bully, Adams, is looking out of his bed real worried, when suddenly Blondie Lawrence, this really pretty boy who looks like a girl, jumps out of the same bed, Adam's bed. I swear. Who gives a tuppenny fuck? Not me. If that's what he likes, fair dues to him. I hope he enjoys it. Blondie's got a lovely arse and looks just like his gorgeous sister who comes to visit on free weekends.

I'm at my bedside locker now and I'm checking my stash and it's nearly fifty quid in English pound notes, all stolen from the old man and he never noticed, the tosser. I'm chatting away to myself like it's normal. 'I'll kill him! This time I will.' I hardly notice that someone's standing right beside me.

'Justin? Old chap?' says Adams, with the smell of Blondie all over him and a sweet tone to his voice. Oh feck off, *old chap*. Can't you see I'm busy?

'You won't tell, will you? *Please?*' Adams begs, all whiny. Jesus bloody Christ haven't I got enough on my fecking plate? Now I'm staring at this whingey fecker and I have yet another of my brilliant ideas.

'One condition?'

'*Anything!*' He's desperate.

In the blink of an eye we're in the school corridor, Adams and I, and it's definitely not allowed and Adams is really, really worried by the illegality of the whole thing. '*Hurry up!*' he says, all panicky. I've got this great big rubber torch I stole from the milking parlour at home and I hope Paddy didn't get the blame. I'm checking all the car keys in the housemaster's cupboard. I'm all dressed of course but Adams is still wearing his dressing gown, just like Noel bloody Coward.

'Got it!' I snatch the car key labelled *Housemaster: white Mini Cooper*.

We're outside now and it's getting a little chilly and I'm balancing on top of a bin cutting telephone wires as Adams holds my waist tightly, from behind.

'Don't get any ideas,' says I.

'You're not my type.'

Jesus! The man's actually got a sense of humour.

Moments later I've got the car started and I'm leaning out the driver's window saying goodbye to someone who is no longer a fat spotty, toffee-nosed English git.

'Thanks a million,' I say. I mean it.

'Montague? I wish I had your nerve.'

'You do Adams, you plonker. You just proved it.' I shake his hand. And now I wish I hadn't shaken it, as I'm not sure where it's been.

'About the other thing …'

'Don't worry, *old chap*. Your secret's safe. You're not the only one, you know.' I wink at him all cool, then I put my foot on the accelerator of the lovely new Mini Cooper and I'm gone down the school drive like Sterling bloody Moss. Christ, this is easier than driving a Massey Ferguson.

Nineteen

A man may die, nations may rise and fall,
but an idea lives on.

John F. Kennedy

Friday, 22 November 1963
Dark clouds fill the sky: a gathering storm. It is early morn-
ing in north Wales, on the island of Anglesey. Huge winter
waves crash against and break over the harbour wall. A sign
reads: 'P&O Ferries. Holyhead to Dun Laoghaire'.

The housemaster's white Mini Cooper, now very dirty,
sits alone at the end of the pier. A Welsh police consta-
ble is writing down the number plate in his black leather
notebook.

At The Hall, on the lawn field, two blanketed race-
horses canter round and round, ridden by Danny Keogh and
another stable lad.

At the church bus stop, Liam, Annie and Maureen Cas-
sidy wait. Beside them is a huge pile of luggage: their worldly
possessions. An old van drives slowly away from the sad
scene. Inside, Donal Sheridan shakes his head, horrified. He
looks in the rear mirror at the people he has just delivered
to the bus for the very last time. He cannot believe what has
happened. And it's all his fault. Nobody has lost their job at

The Hall, ever. The boss man is tough, nobody would dispute that, but he never fires people. It isn't his way.

Donal Sheridan is not an emotional man, but this is just too much to bear. 'Oh what have I done? God forgive me. Where will they live?' Donal decides, at that very moment, that he is going take one hundred pounds from his large savings and send it anonymously to Liam, when Liam finds somewhere to live.

At the bus stop, the Cassidy family are distraught. Annie, wiping tears, clutches something tightly. It is a brown envelope, Justin's letter. She opens the envelope and reads the letter, one more time.

'"Why don't you write, Annie, why? I thought you were my friend." I do, Ma, nearly every day. What's he on about?'

'I don't know, pet. I don't know,' says Maureen.

Annie sobs. Her mother has no words to comfort her. She hugs her daughter tightly, all the same. Liam Cassidy doesn't notice. Liam has aged ten years in the last few days. His world has fallen apart.

At The Hall, as the thunder booms away outside, Bridget Collins enters the dark bedroom, places the wicker breakfast tray by the bed and draws the curtains.

'Good morning, m'lady,' she says, politely.

'I do so love a storm, Bridget. Do you know what I mean?'

'Not really, m'lady. Not really,' says Bridget curtly, unable to hide her hate. She leaves the room, closing the door a little more firmly than normal.

Peculiar girl, says Helen to herself. What is the matter with her? The telephone rings, interrupting her thoughts.

Minutes later, in the dining room, Bobby is eating breakfast and feeding Cromwell bacon. 'There's a good boy. Yes, yes, yes.'

Helen, having dressed quickly, gazes out the dining-room window towards the lawn. She is agitated. The phone call she just received has upset her. Bridget hands her a cup of coffee.

'Thank you,' *says Helen and turns to Bobby.* 'Poor boy. He must have been so upset, and it's all my fault. I didn't even think before I opened my big trap. Do you think he's all right?'

'Of course he is. He's perfectly capable of looking after himself.'

Bridget stares daggers at Helen, then leaves the room with Mary. Helen is so shocked she says nothing. At Charlton, someone would have been instantly dismissed for far less.

'Her eyes. Did you see the look in her eyes?'

'What look?'

'Does everyone hate me?'

'They walked out, for God's sake. We didn't sack them,' *says Bobby.* 'Anyway, I'm not letting that bloody boy ruin our plans, thank you very much. First, I'm taking you, my wonderful wife, to lunch at the Shelbourne.'

'No! The Russell please, darling,' *says Helen, almost too quickly.*

Bobby stares at Helen, surprised. 'Why? You love the Shelbourne.'

'Ah, ha. Oeufs Benedictine, that's why. Haven't had it in ages. If you don't mind, my darling? They don't have them on the menu at the Shelbourne.'

'You are a funny one. All right then, the Russell. And second, the best bit? I've booked tickets in the Pullman seats for the new Western,* How the West Was Won.'

'Wonderful! Are you sure, darling?'

'Never been surer.'

'But Bobby? What if the police call again, or the school?

What kind of a mother would they think me if they find out we are gallivanting around Dublin, when Justin is missing?'

'You're a marvellous mother. Everyone knows. It's hardly your fault the little fucker's turned out completely wild. Now, for once, you'll do what I want. Go and get ready. Go on! Before I change my bloody mind.'

Helen leaves the room, appearing humble, and yet it isn't all an act. During the last few weeks, Helen has started feeling differently about Bobby, because maybe, just maybe, her wild colonial boy is returning after all. What surprises her the most is that she is feeling something she had never thought she would feel again. She is attracted to Bobby for the first time in years.

Bobby puffs out his chest, leans against the mantelpiece, crosses one leg over the other and lights his pipe. He blows smoke, content. Bobby is happy with his newfound courage and thrilled with the way his wife reacted to his advances the night before. Christ alive, he thinks, is that what it was all about? Had I become a wimp, the thing I most despised in all other men? Jesus, I will never, ever, let that happen again.

Cromwell looks up at Bobby and wags his tail.

'Good boy, Cromwell. Good boy. Do you know what? You are my one and only true friend. Good boy. Yes!'

Cromwell jumps up and places his paws on Bobby's chest.

Bobby is delighted. 'Old fool!'

*

It's early afternoon and here I am, riding on top of the 62a bus heading down Aston Quay on my way to Kildare, when I'm supposed to be on a football pitch in Hampshire. Strange as it seems I don't feel worried and I don't feel anxious or nervous or anything. Just a wonderful calm. I don't think I have ever, in my whole life, felt like this. Never. So I start singing. *'I'll tell me ma, when I go home, the boys won't leave the girls alone. They pull my hair, they steal my comb, and that's alright till I ...'*

I'm looking out the window and Holy Mother of God, what do I see? It's the Jaguar, with both the parents, heading into town. Oh thank you, Lord. What a great day. And the best bit? That fecking mongrel Cromwell is in the back. Everything's going *exactly* according to plan.

*

It is dark. Chattering couples stream out of the Savoy cinema. The sign above proclaims: 'How The West Was Won – John Wayne. Gregory Peck. Debbie Reynolds.' Bobby and Helen Montague walk happily, arm in arm, back up O'Connell Street, heading towards Trinity College and then Grafton Street.

Bobby feels this is the best day of his life. His bastard son is fucked. His wife is in love with him again. Incredible. And to cap it all, he's just seen a fantastic new cowboy film that the staff will love when he does a showing in a few weeks' time. That will help them forget all about the unfortunate but necessary departure of the Cassidy family from The Hall.

As they stroll towards the Russell Hotel car park, Bobby also feels a little guilty. He doesn't really want Justin to suffer and he admires the boy's fighting spirit. But then he has to learn, does Justin, like every child. It would never work, him being in love with some bogtrotter. They just wouldn't get along. I am, reasons Bobby, saving Justin from a terrible mistake. Maybe one day he will even thank me for my timely intervention.

On American television, there is a live broadcast. An excited crowd, held back by Dallas police, strain for a view of the most important man in the world. Air Force One, a Boeing 707, is parked at Dallas airport. It bears the seal of the president of The United States of America – an eagle, bearing thirteen arrows in his left talon, and an olive branch of peace in his right.

Jackie Kennedy, the First Lady, appears on the top of the aircraft steps. President Kennedy follows. The American newscaster becomes very excited when he sees them.

'Mrs Kennedy! And the crowd yells. And the president of the United States.'

The president walks down the steps as the newscaster continues. 'I can see his suntan, all the way from here.' Moments later, the president's car moves off.

'The motorcade will head out for downtown Dallas where thousands should already be out on the street right now, waiting for a view of the president and his wife.' The motorcade moves across the tarmac.

One hour later at The Hall, in the back passage, lights are being switched on. Bridget and Mary are doing their rounds, preparing the house for the evening and for the return of the boss man.

'That's odd,' says Bridget to Mary. She has seen a light coming from the gun room and the door is ajar when it's always locked. Now she's worried and she's already convinced there has been a burglary and she'll have to call the guards. Bridget opens the door and peeks inside.

'Oh, Jesus, Mary and Joseph!' Inside, the gun cabinet, oddly, swings open. There are only three guns, not four as there should be. One is missing: Justin's 20-bore. An open

177

box of Eley 20-bore shotgun cartridges lies on the floor,
spilled everywhere.

On the avenue, a stag feeds peacefully on the verge.
Suddenly it looks up, startled, because it has heard rustling
nearby. Alarmed, the stag gallops off through the wood,
running for its life.

The Jaguar turns through the main gateway and onto
the avenue. Inside the car, soft music plays on the radio:
'True Love', sung by Grace Kelly and Bing Crosby. 'Sun-
tanned. Windblown. Honeymooners at last alone. Feeling
far above par, oh how lucky we are. I give to you and you
give to me, true love, true love …'

Bobby and Helen listen to the soothing sounds. Crom-
well is asleep on the back seat. Bobby, totally at ease for
the first time in years, teases Helen. 'I should never have
taken you. Damn Gregory Peck! Too damn smooth for my
liking.'

Helen laughs.

On American television, President Kennedy's motor-
cade makes its way around a bend in Dallas. The police
motorbikes lead. The American newscaster continues: 'The
president's car is now turning onto Elm Street. It'll be only a
matter of minutes before he arrives at the Trademart.'

In the Jaguar, Helen teases Bobby. 'I didn't notice you
exactly dropping off when the ravishing Miss Reynolds
pranced around in that skimpy …'

'Shut up!' interrupts Bobby, staring ahead in disbelief.

'Don't you dare talk to me …'

'Fucking hell!' The Jaguar slows to a halt. They both
stare out, amazed. Cromwell falls off the seat into the rear
footwell, then jumps back up and joins in the staring.

So there I am at last, standing like Wild Bill fucking Hickok. I'm in the middle of the avenue and I've got my legs spread apart and this time the boot's on the other foot, you cunt!

So I yell, just like he always does at me. 'Where *the hell* have you been?'

'Right, *that's it!*' screams the old man and he goes to get out of his shiny car to deal with the situation just like John bloody Wayne. This time he's not going to get away with it.

'Don't you *dare* fucking move, you fucker!' I mean it. I place my shotgun butt neatly up into my shoulder and aim it at the old man and he knows full well that I mean business. I can tell by the nervy look in his eyes. But then the Nazi war criminal ruins this beautiful moment by deciding he's going to get in on the act.

He bounds past the old man and out of the car and stands snarling at me. Quick as a flash, I delve into my left pocket with my left hand, without dropping the gun one little bit. Cromwell knows exactly what I'm after. He stops snarling and starts slobbering in anticipation.

*

The Kennedy motorcade approaches the grassy knoll as the American newscaster continues. 'I was on Simmons Freeway earlier and even the freeway was jam-packed with spectators, waiting their chance to see the president as he made his way towards the Trademart.'

*

Now Cromwell's crunching away at the sugar cubes and I'm still staring daggers at the old man through the sight of my gun through the windshield and he's white as a sheet and it's just brilliant to watch. Brilliant! He's still doing his best, the old man, as he just can't imagine not being in control. 'Put that gun down! Do you hear? Justin? I'm warning you. *Justin!*'

He still scares me, a little. I suppose he always will even after he's dead. But I am not going to weaken, no way, and suddenly something weird happens. The old man weakens himself.

'*Justin?* Come on now. Put it down and I'll explain. It's all for your own good. I promise. Good boy. Your mother and I love you, you know. Really.'

Jesus effing Christ, he's scared, he's actually scared. I've got you, you bastard! Now you know what it feels like, to feel like me. Now I know what it feels like to be in charge. Good God, it's better than sex. Not that I've ever had any. But he's too bloody late with his pleading and he probably doesn't mean it so I just stare straight at him, all cold like, and I pull the gun closer to my shoulder, tucking it in just like he taught me himself, relax my arms, take aim right at the centre of his chest, and begin to squeeze the trigger of the first barrel.

*

The American newscaster is flummoxed. 'It, it, ap ... it appears that something has happened in the motorcade route. Something, I repeat, has happened in the motorcade route. There's numerous people running up the hill alongside Elm Street, there, by the Simmons Freeway. Stand by, just a moment, please. Something has happened in the motorcade route. Stand by, please.'

Twenty

It is a good deed to forget a poor joke.
                                    Brendan Behan

                              Friday, 22 November 1963
I've got all the kit, brushes and oils and rags and I break the
gun into its three parts and start to clean it. The old man
always said that my professional attitude, with my gun han-
dling that is, will stand me in good stead. He's right. I always
feel better when I do it properly. It's cold out here out by the
back steps but I don't mind as I'm a bit hot after all the excitement. I just keep thinking about how, because I didn't chicken
out, I've had the best day of my life. Honest. With the ructions
going on, nobody seems to have noticed I'm here at all.

And look! There's Mary the new girl with her tiny boobs
and she's heading back across the yard towards the house
leading Danny and Paddy Kelly and a couple of the other
lads and she's talking ten to the dozen.

'Bridget told me, so she did. That's who. Bridget. I was
turning down beds. She came running in yelling her lungs
out, "You won't believe what just happened in America!"
Scared the living daylights out of me.'

They rush past me like the north wind without so much
as a glance.

But then Donal appears and he's not moving fast, not even with all the drama. He's from Kerry after all. Donal stops and looks at me. 'Is he dead?' asks Donal, all serious.

'I should *fecking hope* so,' replies I. 'Jesus.'

'That is a terrible thing to say.'

'You're being very pass-remarkable, *Mr* Sheridan. He's hardly a great loss now, is he?'

'May the Good Lord forgive you,' says Donal as he takes off his hat, crosses himself, and walks inside.

So I carry on and wrap the oiled rag onto the long brush and I'm about to shove it into the left barrel, *up its hole*, when who should pop her head round the corner all amazed and flushed is Bridget and her lovely breasts. 'Thank Heavens. You're safe, pet.'

'Oh Bridget, Bridget, Bridget. I missed you Bridge and those lovely bubbly doops.'

I did, really I did. Especially now Annie's had enough of me and can't be bothered to write.

'*Bubbly doops*? What in God's name are bubbly doops?'

She's staring at me like I'm ready for the loony bin at Newtownmountkennedy.

'Justin? Did the boss man see you?'

'He sure did, petal.'

'And?'

'He was a bit sad.'

'You're codding?'

'But then it's not really good to show one's feelings is it, old girl,' I ask in my best English accent, the one I learnt at school.

'Justin, love? What are you on about?'

That fecker Donal, popping his head out the back door, interrupts our lovely conversation.

'Bridget? Hurry! It's on.' Bridget rushes inside. Ah well. That's life.

I just carry on cleaning my gun and start singing to myself, all soft like. '*It's my party and I'll cry if I want to, cry if I want, cry if I want to. You would cry too, if it happened to you. Do, do, do, do, do.*'

*

In the kitchen at The Hall, twenty-five staff, all estate workers, crowd close, listening, on the edge of their seats. The Radio Éireann news journalist speaks through the wireless down a telephone line from America.

'*Here in New York, everybody seems to be stunned and shocked by the terrible news, news that flashed across the United States just over an hour ago.*'

On the avenue the Jaguar rests, engine still purring, headlights still on. The car's wireless is turned up very loud as the Radio Éireann journalist continues.

'*First, the news that an assassination attempt had been made on president Kennedy in that motorcade that we got to know so well in Ireland during the summer, as that motorcade was speeding through Dallas, Texas.*'

Inside the car, Lady Helen Montague listens intently, tears pouring down her cheeks.

'*Then, followed an hour of utter confusion with reports that the president was dead ... the president was alive ... And then, thirty-five minutes after he had been removed from the scene of the shooting to the hospital ...*'

Bobby Montague, sobbing, is slumped on the ground in the middle of the avenue, in the car's bright headlights, covered in blood, cradling the limp corpse of his adored Cromwell.

From the car radio, the broadcast continues.

'*... the news came through that President John Fitzgerald Kennedy ... was dead.*'